Degotoga

Hugh J Willard

DEDICATION

In honor and memory of
Antoinette M. Willard, my mother,
who gifted me with a deep passion for literature

CONTENTS

Foreword

"I regret that the Cherokee east of the Mississippi have not yet determined as a community to remove. How long the personal causes which have heretofore retarded that ultimately inevitable measure will continue to operate I am unable to conjecture. It is certain, however, that delay will bring with it accumulated evils which will render their condition more and more unpleasant. The experience of every year adds to the conviction that emigration, and that alone, can preserve from destruction the remnant of the tribes yet living amongst us." U.S. President Andrew Jackson, from his 6th Annual Message to Congress, December 1, 1834

In 1838 and 1839, as part of Andrew Jackson's Indian Removal Act of 1830, the Cherokee Nation was forced to give up its land east of the Mississippi and to migrate to an area in what is now Oklahoma. The Cherokee called this the "Trail of Tears" because of its devastating effects. They faced hunger, disease and exhaustion on the forced march. Over 4000 of the 15,000 Cherokee died on the Trail.

Chapter 1

"Come 'ere birthday boy, and set on your mama's lap."

Honey slapped her open palms across her bony thighs and bared her crooked, brown-stained teeth through an open mouth. She went back to smacking her chewing gum. "I don't care if you are three times my size. It's your birthday and I wanna hug."

Degu dutifully rose from his cross-legged position on the floor in front of the large screen TV and loped over to her. He was holding a video game controller, dwarfing it in one of his oversized hands. His face held little expression as he gently but awkwardly draped himself across both his mother's legs and half of the light green floral print couch where she sat.

"Ahhh!" Honey squealed before choking out a croup-filled laugh. "Boy, where'd you go and get so big. You was so puny when you come outta me 18 years ago."

She dug her thumb into his waist and twisted it back and forth. "How tall are you now, huh?"

Degu looked down and shrugged.

"Your daddy said he thought you were six feet seven. And you gotta weigh 250, at least."

He shrugged again, reaching up to scratch the side of his head.

"Come 'ere," Honey said, peering through her smudged glasses with a more concentrated look this time. She reached up to examine Degu's head like a chimp grooming her partner. "Let me see how everythin's a doin'."

Degu reluctantly bent his head over toward his mother. She ran her small liver-spotted hands over his scalp. His short black hair was pockmarked with misshapen bald spots that looked like a series of lakes on a map. His scalp was splotchy red.

"Yes. Yes," she muttered. "Your alopecia ain't lookin' too bad. Maybe some of that cream the doctor give you last time is gonna finally work, huh? Whatcha think?"

Degu shrugged once more, still not breaking his downward gaze. He knew his hair loss was worsening, but didn't want talk to about it with his parents. They always seemed too busy entertaining themselves to pay much attention to him.

"Well I think you'll be just fine. Just fine," Honey said before patting him on the back and then pushing him with both hands. "Now you gotta get off before you crush the life outta me."

Degu bent forward and lifted off of his mother. In doing so, he dropped the video controller on the floor. When he bent over to pick it up, his mother smacked him across his backside. "That's one!" she said with her trademark cackling laugh. "You got 17 more to go, and a course, one to grow on," she said wagging her finger at him. "Actually, we'll leave the one to grow on out. You don't need no more growin'."

Degu offered a faint smile and returned to his spot in front of the TV where his new video game, Vision Quest II, was waiting on pause. His parents had given him this birthday present the day before, just after his father, Darrell, received the urgent call to come pick up Degu's grandmother, El-li-si. A neighbor in Shooting Creek, deep in the mountains of North Carolina, called to say that El-li-si's bizarre behaviors were worsening. She had always been considered eccentric within her Cherokee community, but lately she had taken to galloping in circles in her front yard, flailing her outstretched arms, and finally belly flopping onto the ground. Her bobbing head and arms smacking the hard red clay was a disturbing sight to all of her neighbors. The last straw came yesterday when she shaved her head and performed her now daily choreography in the front yard, before finally squatting and peeing on herself.

Degu had only seen his grandmother a few times in his whole life, despite only living four hours away in the small town of Oak Ridge, North Carolina. One of his last memories of her was on his fifth birthday. To the best of anyone's knowledge, she had stopped talking the year before, soon after her husband died. Degu was leery of her, but then again, Degu was leery of most people. She was so different from his parents. They were loud and crass, often laughing and making fun of anyone and anything around them. El-li-si, on the other hand, was mysterious, always staring, always slinking around the edges of any activity.

For his fifth birthday, she brought him a plain brown wooden yo-yo. She didn't say so, but Degu had the gut feeling that his grandfather made it just before his death. When she handed the gift to him, she leaned forward, close to his ear, and through a garbled whisper, said, '*wo-ha-li*'. He was so surprised, he didn't know what to say. When he eventually began playing with the yo-yo, he was startled to hear the word 'wo-ha-li' again, each time he flicked his wrist and unspooled the wooden disc. He only played with the yo-yo a few times before burying it under some dress socks in the top drawer of his dresser. He was too unnerved by his grandmother's whispered remark, and the constant refrain of the word that wheezed in a mystical voice each time he rolled out the toy.

Degu now remembered the yo-yo as he continued playing his new video game, although he couldn't recall the word his grandmother had said to him thirteen years before. He tried to remember his grandfather but was having trouble seeing his face. His attention on the new game didn't help his attempt to see his grandfather once again.

Honey sat with one leg crossed over the other, swinging in a nervous rhythm. The leg motion was out of sync with the more rapid gum chewing and the sharp page turns of the celebrity gossip magazine she was skimming. "Your daddy texted me a little while ago. He and your El-li-si should be here anytime now."

Degu nodded without breaking his focus on the video game.

"I don't know what to expect, son. It sounds like she's finally done gone over the edge. She still don't talk, so I don't know what we'll do with her. We ain't got no more money to put her somewheres so she'll have to stay here. At least for now. You sure you're okay with moving out to your daddy's woodshop in the backyard while El-li-si takes your room? It's supposed to get cold again tonight."

Degu nodded and swung the video controller around while feverishly tapping both oversized thumbs on the forward buttons.

Honey continued talking, never bothering to look up from her magazine. She took one hand off of the magazine and began absently twirling her long brown hair in her fingers. "I reckon we'll all make do. Your daddy and I'll need your help with her. Since he lost his job, he can look after her during the day some while I'm at work, but you'll need to keep her in the afternoons when you get home from school. Your daddy'll need a break, fer sure."

Degu began to nod once more when the horn from the rusted old blue pickup truck sounded in the driveway.

"Ope. There they are. Go help your daddy carry in your El-li-si's things."

Degu hesitated, then dropped the game controller and pushed up on his feet. Before he reached the front door, he caught sight of El-li-si through the curtain-less front bay window. She was prostrate on the ground in the midst of her strange dance. Almost immediately, Darrell was there, bending over and wrestling his mother back up on her feet.

El-li-si continued a modest struggle with Darrell clasping her left arm until they reached the front steps. There Degu opened the weathered whitewashed door and stood, slumped-shouldered in the threshold. She paused and took in the young giant before her. El-li-si was a large woman herself, although the toll of time and heavy labor had stooped her shoulders and compressed her spine. Under her own bald head, she stared out of wide-set black eyes for a moment and licked her cracked, pursed lips as if she might speak. Degu loomed over her and his considerably shorter father. Darrell took advantage of the distraction that Degu's size offered.

"Whuddya think of my boy, Ma? I bet you wasn't spectin' to see somethin' six foot seven and 250 come out from me and Honey." Darrell grinned while pulling off his grimy, oil-stained baseball cap and running his coarse, stubby fingers through his thick black hair. "And look at them arms. The doctor said he got the wingspan of a seven-footer." He was speaking loudly as if his mother were hard of hearing rather than hard of managing reality.

El-li-si opened her mouth and stretched her pallid boney arms forward to embrace her grandson. Degu awkwardly stepped through the doorway and hugged her, seeming to swallow her whole in the process. She pulled back while keeping her left hand on his chest. With her right hand she reached and clasped him around his chin. When Darrell stepped off of the stoop to go pick up her suitcase, she mouthed a word with a thin wisp of air behind it.

"*Wo-ha-li*".

Degu's normally half-slit eyes flashed open at hearing the long lost word. He stepped back from the embrace and stammered. El-li-si reached into the large front pocket of her linen paisley print dress and pulled out a crudely wrapped present the size of a CD. She pressed it against his chest. Degu slowly took the gift from her. He began to utter a thank you when his dad lugged up a large suitcase and a small toiletry bag.

"Son, how about helpin' your old man? I got to go get your grandmother's papers out of the truck. Take these inside, ya hear?"

Degu nodded and started to hold up the present for Darrell to see, but his dad had already turned back toward the driveway. He leaned forward and scooped both pieces in one hand while holding the gift and the door open for his El-li-si with his other.

"Well, looky here. Ain't you a sight, Ms. El-li-si." Honey smiled but didn't get up from the couch. How ya doin', sweetie?"

Like Darrell, she practically yelled her greeting at her mother-in-law. El-li-si's wooden face stared at Honey for a moment while Degu moved over to the side of the couch and set her luggage down.

"Um, no Son," Honey said with a dismissive wave of her hand. "Go take those to your grandmother's room."

Degu put his present on the small side table before picking the bags up and disappearing down the hallway. Just as Darrell stepped into the house, El-li-si shuffled over to where the gift was. She picked it up, marched over to Darrell, and, with a firm, almost fierce face, slapped it against his chest. Darrell's eyes popped open as he slowly lifted his arm to take the forced offering.

El-li-si padded over to the edge of the hallway. Her expression softened a bit. She clapped her hands together twice and watched for Degu to appear through the threshold of the bedroom door. When he did, she regained her determined look and rolled her open palm in a "come here" motion. Moving toward her, Degu felt the subtle rise of caution in his throat. She wrapped both hands around his arm and pulled him over to the couch and down beside her. Honey dropped her magazine in her lap, and raised her eyebrows as they crowded in on her. Her top lip curled up over her open mouth while she readjusted her legs away from El-li-si. She rolled her eyes.

"Well, make yourself right at home, Ma'am."

El-li-si stared at Darrell and pointed at the present he was holding by his side.

"Is this supposed to be for Degu, Ma?" he said, extending the gift in his outstretched hand.

She smacked her hands together, scowled and pointed at Degu.

"Okay, okay. Don't go getting your panties in a wad," he replied, moving over to give Degu the item.

"Darrell Collins!" Honey mocked. "Don't you sass your mama that way," she said, barely repressing a smile. "Bein' full-blooded, she might put one of them Cherokee voodoo spells on you."

Honey pulled in her bottom lip to further stifle a laugh. Both she and Darrell had Cherokee blood, mixed with Irish and Scots-Irish, though neither was ever fastidious in the practices of their tribe's customs and rituals.

El-li-si ignored the two of them, maintaining her focus on Degu, who was fidgeting beside her. While she watched, Degu, despite his best efforts to be careful, clumsily ripped open the wrapping paper. He pulled out a bronze colored home recording CD in a clear plastic sleeve. He held it up to better decipher the black Sharpie scribbling across the top of it. Before he could make out the writing, Honey leaned over El-li-si, to see it for herself.

"THE . . . TRUTH," she drawled. Pulling back to an erect sitting position, Honey pursed her lips. "Oooohh. This sounds serious. Degu, give that to your daddy to put in the CD player. We got to hear this."

This time, Darrell rolled his eyes as he took the CD from his son. He pressed it into the music player, trudged over and plopped down in the tattered brown recliner at the side of the couch. With the flat of his hand pressed against the side of his face, Darrell looked fully prepared to be bored by the contents of the recording.

A slow crescendo of throaty, hypnotic flute and droning drumbeat came into focus before receding behind the baritone voice of the narrator:

"Long, long ago, the earth was in its watery infancy. There were no people and all of the animals lived in the sky, in a home beyond the rainbow. One day when the sky home was becoming too crowded, the animals sent the Beetle to earth to search for land under the waters. The Beetle dove down into the depths of the seas and brought back up mud, which he spread far and wide to create the land. However, the mud was too soft to hold the animals from the sky. So the animals sent the Buzzard down to prepare the land for them. He carried in his beak the original acorn. By the time the Buzzard got to the land, he was very tired; so tired that he flew low. Every time he flapped his wings they hit the ground. With each strike of his wings, mountains and valleys formed. With the last strike, the acorn flew from his mouth and lodged in the soft mud. This would soon become the original oak, the father of all trees. The lands, then floating on the waters, were held in place with four ropes from the sky, two from the sun and two from the moon, representing the four sacred directions. If anything breaks these four ropes, the earth will sink into the waters and it will be as if there never were any lands."

Once the Cherokee creation myth was finished, there was a scratchy, garbled sound, followed by a harsh, high-pitched nasally voice.

"Degotoga, one of the ropes of our family has been severed. We wern't supposed to a done it this way." With that, the recording abruptly ended.

Chapter 2

"Happy birthday to you, cha-cha-cha. Happy birthday to you, cha-cha-cha."

Honey gingerly carried the flat, yellow sheet cake with white and green icing towards the kitchen table. Degu sat at one end, flanked by his father and grandmother. El-li-si stared straight ahead, just over the top of Darrell's head, while her son slouched back in his chair with his hands atop his bulging beer belly.

"Oh, come on Darrell! You got to help me sing. You know your mama don't talk. And I can't carry a tune in a 10-gallon bucket."

Darrell smirked and leaned forward to study the cake that had been placed before them. The flickering flames of two green and white candles held their customary place just above the crude cursive writing that said, 'Happy Birthday Degotoga'. He stared at the dancing lights.

"Sounded like she talked just fine on that CD this afternoon."

"Now Darrell. You don't know that was her on that CD. It was all jumbled and hard to hear. That coulda been anybody."

"Oh, I heard it just fine. Even though we ain't heard her speak in 14 years, who else do you know that knows our son's full name and has an old lady's voice?"

"Well, it don't matter. That's all just gibberish anyways. Right Ms. El-li-si? Those are nice stories and all, but that's all they are," Honey said with a faint smile. "We got more important things to worry about. Like paying bills and getting Degu through his last year of high school. I swear that boy is giving me more gray hairs, and, ooh, Degu, hurry up and blow them candles out! They're making a mess!"

The two candles had burned over half way down, leaving a crooked trail of whitish wax snaking to a clear liquid end over the top edges of the green icing. Degu leaned forward, gave two quick puffs and watched as the white smoke lifted off of the black wicks that glowed orange for a few seconds longer.

"Yea!" Honey chuckled and clapped her hands directly in front of her face. She pulled the two candles out and licked the residual frosting from around the edges. "Let's have some cake!"

Darrell clapped his hands together and rubbed them back and forth, while licking his lips. "I always follow the wife's orders when it comes to eatin'," he said arching his eyebrows. "That, and when she asks for snuggle time."

"Yeah. Them's the only two times you ever listen to me," she replied with an impish grin.

"What else is there? Those are the only things a man needs." Darrell's eyebrows bounced up and down.

"Now, you hush your mouth around your mama and Degu. Or better yet, put some of this cake in it." Honey playfully poked a large chunk on a white plastic fork in his direction. He tilted his head back slightly and opened wide, like a baby bird in the nest. She dropped the piece into his gaping maw, handed one to El-li-si, and then absently pushed another towards Degu. The cake and the small red paper plate nearly slid off of the table.

While Degu and El-li-si ate in silence, the other two continued their prattle. Darrell's speech was muffled by the mouthful of cake. "Did I mention what happened when I first got to Ma's house today?"

"Huh-uh," Honey mumbled through her own closed, bulging mouth.

Darrell swallowed. "I pulled in the driveway and found her banging around on the ground in the front yard. It looked like she'd done it so much that she'd already wore out all the grass in that one spot. It was almost a perfect circle. Anyways, just as soon as I got her up, these teenage boys come ridin' by kinda slow. One of 'em yells out the back window, 'Hey Earth Mother! Tell me how you made the sun and the stars, and I'll show you how I made the moon!' Right about that time, this boy turnt around and stuck his bare ass out the window!"

Darrell slapped his palm on the table, his shoulders shaking from his laughter. At the same time, Honey spit out a small bite of her cake before quickly covering her mouth to stifle both her laugh and the food spew. Degu looked over at his grandmother with concern, feeling increasingly uncomfortable with his parents' ridicule of her. El-li-si sat expressionless, continuing to look straight ahead and taking quick, short chews of her piece of cake.

A few moments later the laughter subsided and Darrell swallowed the last of his bite. He exhaled loudly. "Well, I reckon we need to see about gettin' Ma settled in. Degu, you got what you need out of your room? You set up okay in the shop?"

Degu's mind had been wondering back and forth between seeing his grandmother's crazy dance, her speaking the word 'wo-ha-li', and the words on the CD. With his dad's question, his thoughts fuzzed and dispersed like the smoke rising off of the birthday candles.

He nodded.

"We're gonna catch another cold snap tonight. Why don't you go ahead and crank up the kerosene heater out there so it'll be warm when you go turn in. Especially if you're gonna be sneaking some girls out there later on."

"Darrell Collins! You stop teasing that boy about girls. He wouldn't know the first thing about spendin' time with a young lady. Would ya, Degu?" Honey said in a mewing tone, batting her eyes. "That boy is skeered enough of his own shadow. Besides, I'm sure you got homework to do and things to get ready for the first of the week. Right, Son?"

Without acknowledging either comment, Degu pushed his chair back and rose from the table. On his way to the back door, he paused when he passed his grandmother, offering her a wan smile and slightly raised hand in a gesture of 'good night'. El-li-si maintained her piercing stare and slowly lowered her head.

Once out in the woodshop, Degu leaned against the wide inner sill of the shop's one window. His eyes drifted aimlessly around the yard. School books were stacked, unopened, on his dad's broad table behind him. It was late October and the harvest moon was full and luminous, hanging low in the night sky. Degu felt like he could almost see movement going on under the moon's surface. Without any artificial streetlamps to cut the moon's lighting, he could already make out shadow figures moving over on the far side of the road out around the corner of the house. *Looks like a few young bucks,* Degu thought as he saw the deer gather by the ditch. In the next moment, the deer were illuminated by speeding headlights. Just as the truck was coming into view, one of the deer darted in its path. A brief screeching of tire rubber preceded the thudding crash as the deer was thrown forward into the Collins' front yard. Degu snapped into focus and froze, wondering if the truck driver was okay. He saw the driver get out of the truck, shake his head and raise his arms as he stood over the lifeless form on the ground. The driver slapped his hands on his waist, got back into the truck and drove away.

Degu ran out to where the deer lay. He was not troubled by what he saw. He'd often been hunting with his father and although he never wanted to fire the actual shots, he was not disturbed at the sight of wounded deer. He did, however, feel some relief when his father would put the point of the rifle to the deer's head and pull the trigger. Standing before this young buck, Degu was similarly relieved that it was already dead. When he looked up, he was startled to see El-li-si, holding back the curtain in his bedroom, eyeing him and the fallen buck. He pressed back towards the shop, breaking into a trot to regain the cover of his new sanctuary.

Trying his best to settle, Degu was straining to focus on his American history reading. Again, images of El-li-si rotated in his mind like still shots in his mom's childhood viewfinder toy; first at the front door; then playing the Cherokee creation story, and finally, staring out the bedroom window at him and the freshly killed deer. Soon enough, the strain turned to fatigue. He'd been re-reading the same line in a chapter about the Cherokee Trail of Tears following the Indian Removal Act of 1830, when his face finally thudded directly into the crease of the books binding. The impact barely roused him, just enough for him to lift and cross his arms to create a pillow for laying his head back down on the table.

Around an hour later, Degu woke with a start. He saw that he had wrinkled and ripped a page in his school book. Cursing under his breath, he got up and started scanning the room for scotch tape. Standing by the window, he noticed something jumping and lunging at the deer carcass in the yard. He stood still while his vision adjusted to the level of light offered by the moon, which was now high overhead.

El-li-si?

Degu straggled out the door while pulling on his jacket. Jogging over towards the scene he spied from the shop window, he saw the large silhouette resembling El-li-si dissolving to a smaller, more compact form. He stopped about 10 feet away. Before him was the largest black vulture he had ever seen. The bird was tearing the flesh off of the deer with its strong, severely hooked beak. It paused for a moment and studied Degu, before returning to the task at hand, tearing and yanking another chunk of bloodied flesh and hide into its mouth.

Degu waveringly accepted that he wasn't fully awake when he thought he saw his grandmother scavenging on a carcass. Walking back toward the shop, he scrunched his face, considering why a vulture would be feeding in the middle of the night. When he pushed open the door and stepped into the room, he jumped backwards, banging his shoulder on the heavy wooden door frame.

"Ooof. Grandma! You scared me."

El-li-si leaned back in the chair and began rocking, holding a small burning oil lamp to her side. "That's the first I heard you talk, boy." She bent closer to him. Her voice was reedy but strong. "Degotoga, you got to listen to me good," she said raising her stare and holding motionless for a moment. "You got to come with me. Your brother is in trouble and we got to help him. We got to find him afore more bad stuff happens."

She broke her stare, sat back and returned to rocking.

Degu listed to one side as though he had been tazed. First, his grandmother speaks to him twice in the same day after not speaking for many years, and then she talks crazily about his brother being in trouble. Catching his breath, he took a step further into the room and slowly closed the door.

"El-li-si, what are you talking about? I, I, I don't have a brother. I'm an only child." He noticed blood trailing down the side of his grandmother's mouth. "Grandma, your mouth! You're bleeding!"

El-li-si quickly reached up and wiped off her face. She smeared the blood on the side of her jeans, hastily rose and left the shop, turning off the light on her way out. Degu stood slack-jawed in the dark. He began pacing the room but eventually went and sat on the edge of the cot that was now his bed. The weariness of the day and night was finally setting in his bones. His head was feeling tight and warm, so he lay down and immediately went to sleep.

The next morning, Degu wandered into the house, still hazy from the events of the night before. He was on the cusp of believing that it was all a very bizarre dream. But even as a dream, it was still unsettling to him. He had heard some older Cherokee speak of the power of dreams and the lessons they held. He sat down at the breakfast table with puffy eyes and sunken cheeks. His mom eyed him warily.

"You okay, boy? You don't look so good."

"Uh-huh."

"You didn't sleep good?" she asked, placing a small plate with a fried egg and toast in front of him.

He shook his head before biting into the bread.

Honey sat down next to him and slurped her coffee. She took a long drag from her cigarette while her face sank into a somber tone. Smoke streamed out of her nostrils as she spoke. "I know it's a big disruption having your grandma here. It's a real hassle for all of us, especially your daddy. Just remember, he's got the hardest part. Since I got to go to work and you got to go to school, he'll stay here and watch after her during the day. We just got to be extra helpful with her when we each get home. Maybe you can take her for a walk this afternoon, to give your daddy a break."

"Uh-hum," Degu dutifully answered. He stabbed a section of the egg and slipped it into his mouth. He wondered if his El-li-si would talk to him again that afternoon.

Was it a dream? Did she really say I had a brother in trouble somewhere? He continued mulling over the images from last night while picking at his breakfast.

"Good mornin'!" Darrell called from the hallway where he had his hand wrapped around El-li-si's forearm, escorting her into the kitchen. "How's everybody doin' this mornin'?"

"We're doin'," Honey replied while getting up and setting two more breakfast plates at the table. Despite her instant grin, she jabbed at Darrell. "And stop being so cheerful in the mornin'. I ain't got enough coffee in me yet to take that from you."

She then morphed her smirk into a sugary smile. "Good morning Ms. El-li-si. Come set here and have some breakfast. I got to go in just a minute. Y'all can take care of the cleanup. Darrell, Degu said he'd take El-li-si on a walk this afternoon."

Degu glanced over at El-li-si as she shuffled toward the table to sit. Their eyes met, then Degu looked down. She was wearing a new floral print blouse but had on the same jeans from last night. When she turned to the side to sit, he saw the dark red smear on her pants.

Chapter 3

Degu walked to school most mornings. As the crow flies, his high school was less than a mile through the woods separating his neighborhood from the back side of the school's football stadium. Bright lights and boisterous cheers filled numerous Friday nights in autumn. Degu, however, preferred to sit in his father's old deer stand in the tree line high along the ridge behind the field. The woods abutting the high school campus were no longer available for hunting, which suited Degu just fine. He would rather soak in the solitude from his perch and recreate images of the flora and fauna in his well-worn sketchpad. Among his pencil drawings, his favorites were of the playful antics of the chipmunks scurrying beneath on the forest floor. He had difficulty seeing the small creatures rustling about below, but he could *smell* them as if he were holding them directly under his nose.

When high up in the tree, Degu felt a steadying congruence. During his father's time with the stand, it typically was anchored to a tree at about 20 feet. Degu decided to secure the stand to the highest point he felt still offered stability; in this particular grand old oak, it was latched on at 50 feet. He had slung a thick, knotted rope over the lowest hanging limb. He would clumsily climb up the rope to reach the lowest branch and then scurry up to his refuge. From this position, he could see over the top of the bleacher seats and into the stadium. To the side, he could also see the back of the main classroom building and the steps leading down to the auto shop and carpentry building.

His dad had paid little attention to the care and upkeep of the tree stand, eventually giving it to Degu in a state of shocking disrepair. Degu happily took to the project of fixing the old stand, both functionally and aesthetically. He added vibrant pastel swirls and images of various flying creatures, and lately had begun writing random words in his untutored version of calligraphy. Two days ago, after he heard about his grandmother's antics, he penned the word '*Madness*' in a fashion perpendicular to the existing words '*Roots*' and '*Soaring*'.

Degu paused this morning at the base of the stately old tree and stared up at the stand. He was more jittery than usual. He kept replaying scenes from the day and night before. Each time, his mind's eye would flash to the image of his grandmother's blood-stained jeans; her leaning forward in the chair in the woodshop; her admonishment: 'Your brother is in trouble.'

What was she talking about? Degu's mind skipped. He thought of the word 'Madness'. *What word could I add today?*

He then remembered that he had to go directly home after school to help with El-li-si. The next word would have to wait for another day. Three small chipmunks rose to attention at the base of the trunk but went unnoticed by the gentle giant.

Did I really see her eating the raw flesh of the dead deer? Degu shook his head to clear his mind of the jumble of words and images, and wandered forward towards school.

The carpentry building also housed the offices of the school custodians. After spending most of his school time in self-selected reclusion, Degu had unevenly warmed up to a few of them over the past few months. He liked that they accepted him without question, without gawking at his conspicuous size and harsh and erratic hair loss. He always wore a tattered baseball hat in school to hide his alopecia. Just last week, he took his hat off among them. No one batted an eye.

He also liked that they all seemed comfortable in silence; such a stark contrast to what he experienced at home. As a rule, they were each judicious with their words. The quiet didn't isolate them. Rather, they interacted within the group with a seamless synchronicity. There was a settled feeling for Degu each time he stopped by after school to visit.

Most recently, Degu felt a growing bond with one custodian in particular. His birth name was James Paul but he was dubbed Rojo at an early age due to the bright red color of his hair. He was 19 and had just begun working at the school the month before. Rojo was large, about the same size as Degu. He had closely cropped hair, pale, poor complexion, sallow eyes and a long sharp nose. The two nurtured a kinship borne of social isolation, but also of a shared love of the outdoors. In the past few weeks, Degu had begun dropping by Rojo's tiny closet office in the morning before going to his first period class. Rojo reinforced the routine by having an extra cup of dark roast coffee waiting for him.

In his head, Degu rehearsed telling Rojo about the events of last night. How would his new friend react? Rojo didn't talk much, but he was quite open and transparent with his facial expressions. Degu hadn't known his friend very long, and worried that Rojo would think he was delusional and dismiss his experience. However, he felt like he would burst if he didn't tell Rojo. He just hoped his friend would believe him.

The real issue was that Degu never had a close friend in whom to confide. His "friends" largely existed in the virtual world of video games, wherein Degu would go on missions with others he had met online. Degu was never interested in the violent video games, finally finding his niche with a search and rescue game called Vision Quest. A game that required smarts and intuition over brute force. Through Vision Quest he found a few like-minded people. He had been playing this game throughout his eleventh grade year and was beginning to feel a deeper connection with a few of the other gamers. He liked the anonymity the virtual world afforded him. He felt free to open up and share his thoughts and feelings; certainly a strong contrast from his home. This experience was the closest Degu had come to developing stronger, lasting friendships; until now with Rojo. At least this was a promising start to the friendship.

He arrived at the back of the building. It was a chilly October morning with frost perched along the bottoms of the window panes. Being preoccupied with his thoughts, Degu didn't notice his runny nose or shivering shoulders until now. He quickly grasped the cold steel door handle and hopped inside. Wrapped in a beige wool scarf, Rojo stood in front of him with red cheeks and a smile as he handed Degu the Styrofoam cup of coffee. Degu's big hands swallowed the small cup. He interlaced his fingers around it and held it up to his nose to smell and be warmed by the rising steam. The two shuffled back to Rojo's office to sit for a few minutes. The small laptop sitting on Rojo's desk was playing a YouTube video. Next to the computer was a snarl of cables and an X-Box system.

"That's a cool song. What is it?" Degu asked, trying to sound casual.

"Scar Tissue, by the Red Hot Chili Peppers."

"You hooking up an Xbox here?"

"Yeah. I just moved into my own apartment. I don't make enough money to get cable or the internet, so I plan on spending a lot of time here. I can get online through the school's Wi-Fi."

Degu started to rummage through the video game cartridges in the tattered cardboard box next to the X-Box. He smiled and pulled out the case for Vision Quest II.

Rojo grinned. "Dude, that's my favorite. You play?"

Degu relaxed and nodded. I just got it for my birthday."

"Nice. Happy birthday."

"Thanks."

"Hey, I've got an extra controller. Wanna join me for a new quest?"

"Sure," Degu said.

"I'll have the system ready to go this afternoon. Can you come back by after fourth period?"

Degu's face slumped. "Um, I can't come by after school today." He sat and cast his eyes downward. "I've got to help out with El-li-si. That's my grandmother. She came to live with us yesterday. She's got Alzheimer's or something."

Rojo leaned back in his squeaky, gray metal desk chair. "Wow. Sorry man."

Degu paused and gazed at the computer screen. "Thanks." He put his cup down and rubbed his face and eyes. "There's more to it."

Degu then continued to share the events from last night. He finished just as he heard the bell chime for students to go to their first period class.

Rojo sat forward in his chair. His eyes narrowed. "Well, no offense, but is it possible that you dreamed all of this?"

Degu rose and slung his backpack over his right shoulder, already feeling a bit lighter for having shared his story. "No problem, Rojo. But there is one other thing. This morning, she came into the kitchen wearing the same jeans she had on last night. I saw the blood stain on them."

He turned to walk away, pulling his baseball hat low over his eyes. "I'll catch you later, man."

"Hey, wait a sec." Rojo reached over and pulled out a sheet of paper with some scribblings. "I took some notes on the new VQ II. Maybe you can look over them before we team up." Rojo handed the folded paper to Degu, nodded and shifted back in his chair. Degu was surprised to see a bright glint in his friend's eyes.

"Alright. I guess I'll see you in the morning." Rojo said. He raised his Styrofoam cup. "It'll be another cold one. I'll have the joe ready."

Degu nodded. "Thanks man."

Degu's school routine was well worn. While many of the students, including Degu, had been together for three or more years, few had adjusted to his harsh physical appearance and size. Given his looks and his reserved temperament, his classmates generally left him alone. There did seem to be a residual fear of *catching* his alopecia, as if it were mono or the flu. Degu walking down the hall was like a drop of oil rolling through water. You could *see* the students subtly repelling away from him. The days droned. It wasn't that he was frustrated with the work. He had overheard more than one conversation his mother had with teachers over the years. He *knew* he could easily master the work. It just felt like he was constantly working against the school environment, like the tragic Greek figure Sisyphus pushing the boulder up the hill. The kids weren't the only ones who shunned him. The teachers, despite their best attempts, would eventually show their fears of being around him.

During his 10th grade year, he had a social studies teacher, Ms. Walker, who appeared to be an exception. She took great interest in Degu, even spending time with him after school to help him with his school work. She was probing in a kind way and Degu felt something shifting inside, like a camera lens coming into focus. Here was someone he could trust; someone with whom he could feel safe. One afternoon, Degu was waiting in Ms. Walker's class. She had been delayed with a staff meeting. Her nine year old daughter had walked over from the elementary school. The girl came into the room and was startled when she saw Degu. He smiled and waved. He was not wearing his baseball cap. Panicked, the girl started out of the room and ran headlong into her mother's waist in the hall. '*Mama, he, he scared me!*' In an instant, Ms. Walker's face mirrored her daughter's. She made a small attempt at composing herself before suggesting that Degu go home. From that day forward, his favorite teacher responded to Degu with a cool distance. Once again, Degu reached the top of the hill only to have the heavy stone of human connection roll back down to the bottom.

This particular morning, with the images of the previous night in the fore of his mind, the first two periods seemed to go by in a distorted time warp. When the bell rang and Degu trudged out of class and toward the lunch room, he was surprised to see Rojo standing outside the cafeteria. Usually, Rojo was elsewhere in the building in the middle of the day. He was leaning with one arm propped on the wall, talking with a large African-American girl. The girl was six feet two with dark, blotchy skin and deep, obsidian eyes. Her short hair was pulled back into a tight bob against the back of her head. Degu sidled alongside the pair.

Rojo spied him before he came near. "Hey Bud. I want you to meet someone." He pointed at the girl with his free hand. "Degu, this is Ebony." Looking over her left shoulder, she turned to face Degu. "Ebony, this is my friend, Degu."

Ebony held out a slender hand with unusually long fingers and nails. She smiled. "Hi Degu. It's nice to meet you."

Magic. Instant, unexpected magic.

Time slowed as he reached out in a stuttered motion with his oafish hand. Her grasp was firm but not aggressive. "Ni . . . nice to meet you," he mumbled.

He remembered his alopecia, hidden under his hat and dropped his hand and eyes, but only for a moment. The stirrings he was feeling pushed him, like a salmon charging up a waterfall, to rebuff his shame. He pulled his eyes back up to meet hers.

Rojo spoke. "I was fixing one of the doors on the back hall this morning when I overheard Ebony talking with a guy about playing Vision Quest. They were going into class so I decided to wait to catch up with her after second period. Can you tell her that I'm not a crazy stalker custodian? Degu?"

Degu suddenly realized he was staring at his own reflection in the soft inky well of Ebony's eyes. He felt fuzzy for a moment, like he had dropped into a pit of downy feathers, with some settling in his mouth. He was not breathing, but lingering in his nose was a strong acrid scent that combined with a rich hummus. He scrunched his eyes and broke his sight line to look at Rojo.

"Um, yeah you are. I mean, no. Yeah, it's true, you're okay."

"Ebony just moved here with her family last week," Rojo added.

"Rojo told me you play Vision Quest too. I was surprised to learn that you two play, because most students think it's lame. Not enough abject violence, I guess." Ebony paused and smiled. "Rojo said you two were planning on playing the new VQ II sometime. Can I join you?"

"Um, yeah, sure. OK." Degu felt the temperature rising and the flushing of his cheeks.

Rojo noticed his friend's embarrassment and interjected. "Maybe we can play tomorrow after school. I found this one quest that involves these bizarre looking creatures from the Spirit World. Don't know yet if they're good or evil. Maybe the three of us can take on the challenge and find out."

Ebony smiled. "Sounds great to me. I haven't seen that one yet."

Just as Degu was regaining some equilibrium on the outer edges of the conversation, Ebony pulled him back in. "Your name is really different. I like it."

Without taking time to think, Degu blurted, "That's just what my parents started calling me. My grandfather gave me my real name. It's Degotogo. It's, it's—"

"Cherokee," she interrupted with an admiring expression. "It means . . . standing together, I think."

"Um, yeah. But how did you—?"

"My grandmother is Cherokee. Her great-grandmother made the Trail of Tears journey as a little girl from the mountains of North Carolina to Oklahoma back in the 1830's.

Degu stood mute. He was trying to absorb the details of Ebony's brief family history while feeling a soft burning in his chest. Degu sensed that Ebony was much more attuned to her Cherokee heritage than he was to his own.

While he processed all of this, Ebony spoke. "So are you Cherokee too, Degu?"

"Uh, yeah, some. My grandmother is full blood. But I don't know that much about her. I hadn't seen her since I was five . . . until yesterday." Degu stole a look over at Rojo. "She just came to live with us."

"That's cool. Maybe you'll learn more now." Ebony's smile was comfortable and inviting.

"Well, I've got to get back to my office to get more cleaning supplies," Rojo said. "It was nice to meet you, Ebony." Rojo shot a look at his friend. "Maybe Degu can get your number so we can plan to play VQ II tomorrow."

Degu blushed again.

"Would you like to join me for lunch?" Ebony asked.

Degu wheezed his response. "OK."

Ebony ambled into the lunchroom with Degu lumbering slightly behind, over to an open table. He sat stiffly, unsure of what to say, when Ebony asked him about his grandmother. "So, tell me more about your grandmother."

Degu studied the floor for a moment. "She's, um, she's got some kind of mental problems."

Ebony had just taken a large bite of her sandwich. Her cheek stuffed with roast beef, she slowly nodded, held her hand up to cover her mouth and offered a muffled "I'm sorry." She then swallowed and asked softly through the remaining bulge in her cheek, "Is she okay?"

Hearing the care in Ebony's tone was unsettling to Degu. He was feeling residual agitation in recalling the bizarre events from yesterday afternoon and evening. Ebony asking the question only served to stir this discord further. And yet, he continued to feel an odd warmth while being in her presence. *Is it my imagination or is she interested in me?*

"Degu? I hope I'm not being too forward in asking?" Ebony's dark eyes were like a cool, viscous salve to his fevered state, advancing slow and steady, descending into his throat and chest.

"No. It's okay. She's, um, we don't know what all is happening. My dad just brought her home yesterday."

"Oh, I'm sorry to hear." Ebony pulled back in her chair and straightened her spine. She then cautiously continued. "You know there are a lot of indigenous peoples who don't even acknowledge that there are mental problems. They believe that it's all spiritual. It's all about our interconnectedness and balance; with each other, with all of life and nature."

Degu's mind swirled as he attempted to focus on what Ebony was saying. The word 'interconnected' jarred him, so that he heard his grandmother's voice again. *One of the ropes of our family has been severed. Your brother is in trouble.*

While Ebony continued her musings about the sources of mental and spiritual illness, her speech receded away from the pitching volume of El-li-si's voice in Degu's mind. He began to grimace as if he were bracing against a quick rising migraine headache. He brought the index and middle fingers of both hands to the sides of his temples and started to push in with a circular motion. A din swelled on the far side of the cafeteria near the windows. Students began thrusting their chairs back and clambering over each other to see something outside. The cafeteria windows framed the back of the school facing the carpentry building and the football field. Ebony stopped and peered over the top of Degu as she rotated in her seat to see what the matter was. Degu rose half way from his chair and turned when he heard a shrill voice of another student over the commotion.

"What's that crazy old lady doing?!"

In the ensuing laughter, Degu knew it was his grandmother. He shoved his chair back and stumbled as he lunged towards the gathering crowd. His hat fell to the floor. He froze and looked back at Ebony. She was staring at his head. Degu turned forward and ran to the back edge of the students.

Given his height, he could see relatively easily over the other students. Still, he lifted onto his toes, craned his neck and squinted, trying to focus on where his grandmother was. With all of the clatter, none of the students repelled away from Degu when he pressed into the crowd. He instinctively knew she must be flailing on the ground, doing her "crazy dance". Within a few moments, his intuition was confirmed. There, on the crinkly beige autumn grass, his El-li-si was teetering and slapping her arms and legs on the cold, hard ground.

Chapter 4

Degu felt a surge of panic. He swiveled, pushed out of the back of the crowd, and, without stopping to say anything to Ebony, ran to the emergency exit door at the far end of the cafeteria. When he burst outdoors, the alarm sounded, alternating in cadence with a flashing red light. The alarm was severe and angry, like the harsh honking of a Canadian goose at 100 decibels. Degu crossed the threshold, and looking up, saw El-li-si running towards the woods. A moment later, Rojo came into view in the distance, which caused Degu to pause. His friend was chasing after her as she descended into the woods. Degu joined the pursuit from the rear.

He was already panting as he approached the entrance to the woods. There was only one path through to the other side, which led directly to Degu's house. It wound down a knobby slope and curved to the left, ascending again up and around the large oak tree that was Degu's second home. He had lost sight of both El-li-si and Rojo when he reached the dry creek bed that creased the bottom of the small ravine. He looked up and stopped in his tracks. Where the hulking oak tree had once blotted out the skyline from this vantage point, there was now the bright sun, so searing and full that it fogged the surrounding air with a dusty white reflection. The tree was gone.

The whole of this experience came over him in a wave of vertigo. Beginning with his grandmother's arrival yesterday, leading through to her crazy dance at school and now the abrupt demise of his beloved sanctuary, Degu was swept up in a surreal haze. He shook his head violently side to side while bending over with his hands braced on his knees. Large plumes of mist shot from his open mouth into the still, cold air.

After pulling his thick hand down across his face to clear away the sweat, he took one more quick breath and pushed up the hill. He halted again when he arrived at the fallen tree and the massive maw that was the underside of the oak tree's root ball. There before him, hanging from the damp black tentacles of shredded roots, were El-li-si and Rojo's clothes! Degu spun around and surveyed the immediate surroundings. The running had quelled the surge of panic he first felt in the cafeteria. But now seeing the clothes and not seeing any other signs of the two, Degu felt it return, stabbing him like a lightning strike. He thrust his chest forward and pulled his outstretched arms behind him. Just as he was beginning to release a deep, guttural scream, his bellow was blunted by the croak of the largest bullfrog he had ever seen. The bluish-gray creature was sitting down in the gullet that was created by the tree's fall. An underground spring was gurgling up in the crater. Degu's eyes widen as he stared into the clearest, dark green water.

How is this possible? he thought, continuing to stare. *The water is so dark and yet I can see through it!* Leaning forward to get a closer view, he saw the flopping soles of two sets of bare feet that must have been 20 feet below the surface of the water.

"El-li-si! Rojo! What are you doing?!" Degu grimaced and straightened his back. "They're gonna die!" he shouted to the faceless woods.

Degu had never learned to swim. He was self-conscious enough being fully clothed. He never had the mettle to withstand the added scrutiny he knew he would receive being so big and having alopecia. Degu now stood before this inexplicable pool of water watching his grandmother and first real friend, descending further and further, to what he was sure would be their deaths. He sat down next to the edge of the water and began sobbing. He wrapped his enormous hands over his face and moaned.

In the midst of a heaving, staccato breath, the bullfrog jumped up onto Degu's lap. Its bumpy skin was cool, rubbery and slightly gummy. The frog croaked again and then turned and splashed into the middle of the pool. It circled just under the surface and kicked up and out of the water with enough force to return to the same spot on Degu's lap. Degu paused his wailing and looked at the creature. He was stunned to see sitting atop the wide mouth and flared nostrils were bulging *human* eyes, deep amber colored irises flecked with black. The eyes were searing and pleading at the same time. The frog repeated the process, diving again into the water and returning to Degu's lap.

This happened a third time before Degu finally spoke. "You, you want me to follow you into the water? But I can't swim. I can't. I don't know how . . . I . . . I . . ."

This time the frog lunged up into Degu's face. It slapped its bulbous body hard against him causing him to fall backwards. He had been sitting on the very rim of the ground leading to the spring. He slipped down the bank and into the water, yelping as he sluiced into the pool. Dropping below the surface, he was surprised that his grief and panic were replaced with the thought of how warm the water was. It was October and the past several nights had been quite cold. Here he was, surely descending to his death, like his grandmother and Rojo before him, and all he could think of was how good the water felt.

The inviting taste on his tongue was one of butter and salt. He closed his eyes and then realized that he was still breathing! His breaths slowed and leveled, and he began to have the most amazing and curious memories. He opened his eyes and recognized that he was in his mother's womb.

He had returned to his first home, the purest definition of peace and innocence and security. Degu noticed that there was a natural light around him although he could not find its source. In slow motion, he curled into a fetal position, brought his thumb into his mouth and looked above. Through the thick membrane of his mother's uterus, he could faintly detect a deep blue light through a translucent, misshapen ball covered in spidery veins. It was throbbing in a steady and calming cadence. Ba-bump, ba-bump, ba-bump.

That's my mother's heart! Is this what death feels like? It's so peaceful. Why are we all so afraid of it? Death is just coming home again. Degu closed his eyes, smiled and rotated in the warm, sweet water.

When he opened his eyes, he was shocked to see a monstrous face inches from his own. Degu's scream was garbled. He tried to recoil but there was nowhere to go. The water felt much more viscous. His yell caused the freak to open its big, bowed eyes. In an instant, Degu saw himself in this thing's eyes. He was confused and terrified.

Are you my brother? Are, are you my twin?

The creature's face was disfigured. There was an open crevice from just off-center of his top lip up through his malformed nose. Flesh dripped loose from the sides of the cleft lip. His forehead was protruding with his crooked eyebrows resting underneath. Despite this, the other child smiled and gently reached towards Degu with an open hand containing only two fingers and one stub.

Degu felt nauseous, but could not take his eyes off of the harsh figure before him. The water thinned and the being impulsively grabbed Degu's hand. Degu felt a cold shiver through his body. He was fighting to gain some sense of equilibrium. He attempted to speak but the water filled his mouth and lungs, making this impossible. Still having his brother's hand clasped around his own, Degu thought, *What happened to you?* The smile on his brother's distorted face slackened, closing much of the wide gap in the cleft. He looked down but gave no response. With the abrupt change, Degu jerked his hand free and pulled it in close to his own chest.

What, what is your name? What happened to you!?

When Degu pressed these thoughts towards his brother, the twin reached his hand forward once more towards Degu's face. While his brother maintained his downward stare, Degu sensed a phrase, a name coming toward him.

"Wo-ha-li".

As soon as Degu absorbed the name, there was a violent force, a powerful, contracting vacuum sucking Degu backwards and away from his brother. The water thinned to the point of feeling more like a hot gas. In the next moment, Degu's head thrust up and out of the pool. His lungs were suddenly clear and he gulped in the dry, cooler air. He flailed his arms onto the hard red clay bank of the water's edge and pulled himself up onto solid ground. He rolled over on his back and heaved for several minutes. His head ached from the unrelenting pressure just inside the edges of his skull.

Chapter 5

Once his breathing leveled, Degu scrunched his eyes closed before opening them and shaking his head. *I just met my brother!*

The words seared in his mind, causing a sharp pain to form out of the dull ache, rising to the crown of his head. He brought his hands to his head to tamp down the hurt. His vision cleared. In spite of the pain, Degu rolled over onto his stomach and planted his arms and hands by his sides, preparing to push himself up. Completing the roll and lift, he came face to face with a large animal's skull.

"Ahhh!!!"

Degu hurtled sideways and onto his back, pushing with his legs to increase the distance between him and the symbol of death. At the last moment, Degu realized his was going to fall back into the underground spring. He whipped around to catch himself before dropping into the water, only to plant his face in scratchy, yellowing meadow grass. The spring was gone! He spun again in the opposite direction, now on his hands and knees, and stared at the ominous face sitting placidly at an angle to Degu. Frozen, he observed the various cracks that meandered through the dirty white boney structure. The lines ran a course around the deep and perfectly round eye sockets and down to the hooked, yellowed ends of the snout. The long skull reminded Degu of a picture he had seen somewhere of a giant bird man.

Degu gulped in a breath and continued to look at the head. In time, his breathing returned to normal as he assessed that this thing was no immediate threat. He sat back and wrapped his arms around his bended knees. He started to rock slowly back and forth, trying to understand all that had just occurred. Despite feeling calmer, he was still dazed. Eventually, he lowered his head onto his crossed arms.

Degu felt the warmth of the sun on the back of his neck and for the first time realized that his clothes were perfectly dry. When he looked, he found that he wasn't even wearing the same clothes he had put on in the morning! His faded blue hoody and brown faux leather jacket were gone, and the dinghy plain red tee shirt was replaced with a fresh, bright white one. Degu rubbed his hands across the cool soft cotton tee and then down to the new black jeans he was wearing. He noticed a small bump in the front right pocket of the pants, reached in and felt the smooth, round object. He pulled out the toy yo-yo of his childhood, the gift from his grandfather. He stared at it. He noticed that it glistened and was smaller than he had remembered. It was still the same medium brown color but had a glossier sheen. He turned it over and began to loosen the slip knot to place it on his middle finger. He was surprised the string loop fit.

Before he extended his arm to toss down the yo-yo, Degu jerked when he heard the sharp, shrill voices of a middle aged man and woman. The sounds were coming from off the ground, near the edge of the wood line. All he saw were two oversized ravens sitting a third of the way up in a large oak tree. An oak that looked identical to his favorite tree back in Oak Ridge. Degu stared for several moments at these slick black birds. They had dusty gray heads with ice blue eyes and were the size of German shepherds. He was surprised to feel a mixture of connection and anger towards these creatures he had never before seen.

"They talk a lot but seldom have anything of value to say. Because of this, their kind is often the unwitting hosts of the Raven Mocker."

Degu whipped his head in the direction of a booming new voice, which was were the skull had been. He was startled to find the skull was no longer there.

The sound swung to the opposite side. "There are more and more spirit animals who are losing their capacity to speak in both human and their own native tongue."

This time, when the baritone voice was in mid-sentence, Degu spun around to find the skull was now atop a hulking body, standing behind him. With one shiny metal wing and one arm by its sides, the beast's ochre skin was coarse with open, oozing pustules and patchy tumbleweeds of black hair. The skull remained unadorned, with no other discernible features. When it spoke again, Degu watched the long slender jaw bones and hooked beak open and close.

"The blackbird is a poor man's buzzard. While the buzzard is quietly doing her job, the raven is busy complaining, or worse, ridiculing others." The creature pointed up at the birds with its formidable wing before continuing. "Sometimes the Raven Mocker comes and inhabits the bodies of the weaker of this kind."

Degu rose to his feet, feeling self-conscious. The fear he had felt was now highlighted with an awareness that he stood before a powerful benighted presence. He wiped his dirty hands on the backside of his jeans and then dusted off the front of his tee shirt. He reached for his head to cover his bald patches and was surprised to realize that his hair was now almost all gone; only a few random wisps remained. He dropped his hands to his sides and looked back at the freakish, regal being in front of him.

Caw!!! Caw!! Caw!

The ravens lifted from their perch and shot between Degu and the beast before veering to the left. Their black wings had an oily green sheen that reflected a prism as they flew. The pair continued to screech while ascending and receding into the distance. Again, Degu returned his gaze to the presence before him.

"The Raven is your kin, Degotoga. But those two are not here to help you. Oh, they have their moments. They can be clever and charming, but ultimately, these blackbirds are far too vain and small of spirit to provide for you on your quest. And there is the issue of the Raven Mocker." The beast turned it's skull to the side before looking skyward. "Your support lay elsewhere, here in the *adanvado e lo hi*. You would call this 'Spirit World'."

Degu continued to stare straight ahead at the figure before him. He mouthed a half-formed syllable, trying to orient to this majestic, faceless force. His word was inaudible.

The hollowed eye sockets fixed back on Degu. "You will need your voice for this part of the journey, young one. You won't always have it. Eventually you will find your place in the language of silence, the authentic language of your spirit animal. But until that time, it will be necessary for you to claim your human voice; to learn when and how to use it. The equilibrium of our sacred world is no more in these days. There has been disruption coming from the other side. While this has always been true, there is a different character to this opposing, material energy. A time of reckoning may be drawing near. You have been called here for a noble purpose, Degotoga. It is time that you forsake your wounds from the new world, the world of your human birth. One of our great elders is *E Do Da*. In the new world you knew him as Nelson Mandela. He spoke of no passion being found in being small. You will encounter many opportunities to choose between smallness and light, between inauthentic fear and the love of your imperfect community. Consider well, young brave. Choose your guides with great care. Go and find your *Wohali*."

Degu's eyes widened at the last word; the one he first heard at age five, uttered by his grandmother; the one he had now heard twice more in the past 24 hours, including by the disfigured face he had been next to in the womb of the underground spring.

"Wohali is my brother. But he is a, a . . ."

Degu paused when he realized he was speaking aloud. Having turned his gaze inward as he thought of his brother, Degu now returned to focus on the skull-headed creature. Looking up, he saw the beast had vanished. There was no trace of the hulking body or the enigmatic skull that sat fixed on its massive shoulders.

Degu stood stock still. *Where am I? Is this all an illusion? A dream? Even if it is a dream, is it the vision experience of my Cherokee ancestors? Was there truth in the womb? In the shamanic bird-skull man?*

He felt a warm breeze course across his torso and head. He heard newly unfurled leaves slap one another in the branches above in a light and playful choreography designed by the same breeze. It was springtime in this world. *But why is the grass withering?* He was aware of the absence of moving air across his lower legs and feet. While puzzling about these things, he looked up. Through the giant pines and assorted hardwoods, a shaft of light cut a path from the sun to the ground. The beam seemed to curve slightly and light in a perfect circle in the meadow grass about 30 yards away from where Degu stood. He peered upwards again, this time his sight drawn to two large silhouettes perched in the oak tree where the ravens were moments before. They sat silently on a broken branch that Degu recognized. That was where his dad's tree stand was mounted on the tree back home. He knew them to be vultures, but from this distance was unable to determine anything more about them.

Suddenly a faint din began increasing in volume. The air filled with grunts and hums. Degu quickly detected a stale fungal odor. Before seeing the source of the sounds and smell, the odor pitched to a high acridity, burning inside Degu's nostrils. He saw a low level dust cloud, out of which came a charging horde of unidentifiable animals. Dirty pink colored snail-like cylindrical bodies without faces were rushing forward en masse on four short, muscular *human* legs and porcine hooves.

Panicked, Degu ran in the opposite direction. He had not gotten very far before he saw what looked like three pale green inchworms coming towards him, only these were three feet tall and they had human ears on the sides of their heads. Their undulating strides were covering large swaths of ground rapidly. And with each stride, they doubled in size. With creatures coming from both directions, Degu instinctively turned and headed toward the wood line for shelter. Within ten yards of the dark refuge, he came to a stumbling halt. Two large yellow slit eyes, the size of cantaloupes, were blinking erratically, and moving in a zigzag motion towards him. Not waiting to see what those eyes were attached to, Degu shifted and ran to the right, in the direction of the circle formed by the bending shaft of light. When he arrived in the center of the light, he again stopped.

The adrenaline continued to thrum through his body, up through the temples on each side of his head. Looking up into the light, Degu squinted to see that the two vultures had soared upwards. They were gliding lazily at the edges of the light. Suddenly Degu lowered his stare and grew still. With the oversized inchworms and the other creatures nearly upon him, Degu thrust his long, lumbering arms around him in one arcing sweep and shouted.

"ENOUGH!"

His voice had a force that bellowed from deep within. It felt like he had just expelled high grade sandpaper out of his throat. Never before had Degu yelled in his life. The experience startled him. At first, he didn't realize that all of the creatures stood still about him. There was no movement, save for the hard panting of the quadruped snail creatures. Their slimy skins glistened in the light while their whole bodies pulsed.

In the vacuum of sound and movement that followed, yellow ovoids from the woods came prancing out into the clearing. Rather than being the jaundiced eyes of some terrific beast, these eyes were held aloft by thin green vines, about four feet high, that curved down to tufts of light brown roots at the base. These fanciful beings more danced than ran. Seemingly unbothered by Degu's booming command, they tottered forward and surrounded him like excited children. They began a harmonic hum that instantly soothed Degu. He felt the pain in his throat melt as if he were swallowing a cool, thick malt drink. The adrenaline-laced tension similarly flowed away from his temples, neck and shoulders. His whole body relaxed.

At that very moment, he remembered El-li-si and Rojo, and their descent into the spring. Standing amidst the gathering of strange beings, Degu strained to search the greater area for El-li-si and Rojo. The snail creatures were now statue still while the ovoids bobbed and the giant inchworms swayed in place. He peered over the tops of the snails backs across the grassy plain into the distance. One of the vultures that previously soared overhead was now gliding lower in the distance, nearly coming into contact with the ground at the edge of the horizon. Near the bird, a weathered gray stallion galloped.

Cawwwwwwarrrrrrgggghhhhh! Caw! Caw!

Degu twitched and looked over towards the large oak. The oversized ravens were back on their roost. Again, he felt an odd mix of familiarity and annoyance.

He returned his sight to the horizon at the edge of the field. The vulture and horse were gone but, *El-li-si!* . . . *And?* Degu saw the backs of his grandmother and another person running in the distance. He could see it wasn't Rojo. It was difficult to make out anything about this other person beyond his size. He was about the same height as El-li-si, but with broad, albeit stooped, shoulders and long boney arms. His bald head suggested advanced age, with large discolored liver spots, visible even from a long distance. Both were wearing sleeveless black gowns that flapped loosely in the breeze.

I've got to get to them! Degu thought as he pushed furtively through the mass of creatures. He wanted to keep his eyes on the pair, but needed to look down to negotiate his way through the crowd. When he looked up again, they were gone. Degu's shoulders dropped. He knew they were too far away. He would never catch them. *Where are they going?*

With arms swinging and slapping his sides, Degu made his way over to the base of the oak tree. He thudded as he sat down, back against the massive trunk. The foreign creatures were all still now, staying in place on the field, surrounding the clear circle of sunlight in the center. They stared solemnly at Degu who sat with his hands covering his face.

"Well, at least I know that El-li-si is alive, and—"

Caaaawwwww! Caaa—

"YOU SHUT YOUR . . ."

Degu's face burned as he glared up above him at the two blackbirds. He swallowed his remaining words and groaned in a grading low pitch while wrapping his forearms around his head. Twice, in the span of a few moments, he had reached a decibel level four times louder than he had ever spoken in his life. It felt like projectile vomiting, leaving him exhausted. "This is insane. I can't believe this is happening. Who was that old man, and where is Rojo? This can't be real."

Degu dropped his tired head back into his hands once more. This time he was aware of the cool, slick veneer and the small but bulky form of the wooden yo-yo pressing into his cheek. He pulled his hand away from his face, and studied the toy. He remembered his brother's name being released each time he had played with it as a child. Degu was confused at the urge he suddenly felt to hear it again; *Wohali*, his newfound brother's name. He stretched his arm but then realized he needed to stand to allow the yo-yo to fully extend. When he rose from his seated position, all of the creatures' eyes lifted and remained trained on him. He was no longer afraid of them. He paused, looking back and forth from the strange animals to the toy, and then gently allowed the wooden cylinder to roll off of his finger.

At first, there was no perceptible sound, although the ears of the faceless quadruped snails lowered submissively and the inchworms and ovoids bowed reverently. Degu flicked his wrist and the yo-yo climbed back up the string.

Nothing.

He grasped it, and then released it again. This time he could hear a faint refrain: *The time has come.*

Degu straightened his back and cut his eyes to one side and then the other. Another release of the toy down the string. This time on the way down, *The time has come. Wohali awaits;* and on the way up, *Find me, know Wohali.*

Degu jerked his head down and stared at the yo-yo he now held in his palm. He lifted it in the flat of his hand to eye level and squinted as if he would discover the source of its magic in the narrow recess that split the two wooden halves. It really was a most ordinary toy, although when Degu lowered it slightly and looked on the surface of the visible side, he was drawn to the curved black lines that looked like the remnants of ocean waves having lapped on the shore. *This looks like the lines of a tree,* he thought. *This really is made of wood. Maybe it—*

Caaawwww! Caaawwww!

Degu's thoughts were interrupted again by the screams of the birds. The two ravens tore from their roost above, hurtling down at him like kamikaze pilots. At the last moment, Degu raised his forearm over his face. The first bird's beak stabbed into the flesh of his hand. Degu's fingers spasmed, causing the yo-yo to fly freely into the air. The second one speared its beak through the yo-yo's loosed knot. The pair then turned and sped off, rising over the animal multitude, and disappearing beyond the distant plain with the yo-yo dangling behind.

Degu winced and grabbed his wounded hand. There was more

bruising than actual blood. He stuck the hand under his other arm against his side and walked in a tight circle. He heard a growing clamor around him. All of the beings that had gathered were now becoming agitated. The snails were snorting and clomping their hooves at the ground, while the giant inchworms were writhing and contracting into smaller, pallid forms. The ovoids were swinging harshly in uneven ellipticals, devoid of any joy they had expressed just moments before.

Degu was puzzled by the change in the animals' demeanor. He began to wonder if the snail creatures would turn and attack him. He pulled his throbbing hand from his side and flexed it to see how useful it would be if he had to defend himself. He began to drag his feet backwards and away from the crescendo of the disturbed beings, although they turned and began to move towards him.

"Step into the circle of light."

Degu stopped, turned and looked up. Above him, on the roost where the ravens previously sat, was the one remaining turkey vulture. The beast spread his two-toned black and gray wings and thrust them back into a resting position.

"Hurry Degotoga!" the bird hissed. "These creatures are confused and unstable. They will still respect the light though."

Degu moved his eyes over toward the circle of light. It was smaller than it was a few minutes before. On one side, the snail creatures were still stomping the ground and banging into one another. There was a clear path between them and the inchworms. The worms had now reduced all the way down to their original size of three feet. The ovoids had collapsed and were lying with crooked stems on withered grass. Degu surged forward toward the lighted circle. None of the animals seemed to notice as he ran and tripped. His outstretched arms and large frame smacked the earth and he slid the final few feet into the center of the circle. The vulture spread his massive wings and, without flapping, glided down and lit next to Degu's face. It was much larger than Degu realized.

Degu pushed up to a seated posture. His dull eyes now trained on the giant bird before him. "How do you know my name?"

The bird cocked his head slightly to one side. His wrinkled red crown was sparsely covered with wiry black hair, reminding Degu of his own alopecia. His hollowed eyes transfixed Degu. The bird twitched, breaking Degu's spellbound gaze.

Degu blinked and shook his head. "And how is it you can talk? You're a buzzard. You hardly make any sounds at all."

Lifting one clawed foot slightly and stepping closer to Degu, the bird spoke once more. "In your world, no, my kin do not talk. Here in the Adanvado I have been given few words. I must be wise and deliberate in how I expend them."

The vulture rotated to the side and looked over the other animals to the field beyond. "Your quest is before you, Degotoga. I can guide you if you so choose. The other animals will disperse soon enough. I suggest you rest here for a while."

With those words, the giant bird spread and held his wings apart while running and finally lifting off. He swooped up, curved, and returned to his roost in the big oak at the edge of the woods.

Degu was glad for the suggestion of rest. Weariness from the morning's events was already seeping into his bones. He stuttered back down to a prone position, laid his head on his outstretched arm, and quickly dropped into a deep sleep.

Chapter 6

Degu realized he was walking along a wide dirt path in the late afternoon. He was tired and dirty, his clothes were soaked in sweat. He rounded a bend in the tree-lined path and came into a clearing. On his right, Degu saw the largest oak tree on a small island in the center of a small lake. It was flush with deep green leaves and resembled the tree from home in almost every way. The difference was that this one reached to the sky. While taking in the enormous presence of the tree, Degu heard the rumble of hooves. The rhythm was quick but solid and deliberate. He turned to face the opposite side of the path. Before him lay a wide pasture with soft tan wheat grasses. A three-line barbed wire fence separated Degu from the field. The stallion that he had seen earlier was charging toward the fence and him. Degu flinched and ducked with the massive silver steed upon him, still at full speed. It stopped in an instant, inches from the rusted brown wire. The dust and air thrust forward over the horse, and splashed Degu. He uncurled and stood erect, staring at the beast. The animal's eyes were kind and wise. The large black holes of his nostrils perspired and throbbed. He shook his head, hurtling spit to each side. Degu stepped forward, reaching out his flat hand, to touch the animal.

Just before making contact, a high pitched buzz began emanating out of a cloud of steam rising off of the lake. In an instant, the lake water evaporated, leaving a horde of tiny black and red bugs scurrying along the drying lake bed. The horse leapt over the fence, over Degu, and shot forward. Degu turned to see millions of the bugs in a frenzied swirl around the trunk, ascending the tree like an erupting geyser. They made a piercing sound which pitched higher as the bugs swarmed the entirety of the tree all the way skyward. They glowed and pulsed like a burning ember being fed by air.

The horse bounded and disappeared directly into the center of the insects, right where the massive tree trunk should have been. The next moment, he reappeared out of the back side, with a chunk of wood in his mouth. He immediately cut hard to his left and sped off. As quickly as the red and black mass rose to the heavens, the chaotic creature column fell back to the ground. In its wake was nothingness. The lurid insects had consumed the whole tree. The sound retreated down to a lower pitch with the bugs trailing away in the distance.

In the absence of sound that followed, Degu stood dumbfounded. After a moment, he began calling out. "What happened here?! This is all wrong! The tree! The tree! No! It shouldn't . . ."

Hearing a rustling in the shrubs along the path, he turned to see large dark eyes peering out from behind a large bush. These eyes were timid, almost expressing fright. Degu took a few small steps in their direction. Slowly they moved out of the shadows, and claimed their place on a face coming into full view.

"Ebony! What are you doing . . . how did you get here?"

"Degu! Take my hand," she pleaded, extending both arms while moving toward him. "You must leave the dream now and come with me. I'm here."

Degu's vision went dark and then reemerged blurred, everything appearing as though through a film of Vaseline. He blinked a few times and his sight cleared.

"I'm here, Degu." The voice was soft and sure. Ebony's arms were still extended, pulling Degu in her direction, out of the dream.

Degu stared blankly, first at Ebony, and then at his surroundings. He was back in the circle of light. The oak tree where the giant ravens, and then later the turkey vulture had roosted, was to the left. The odd assortment of creatures was now gone; the field appeared to be untrodden.

"Degu."

He turned back to look at Ebony. He drank in her deep, dark and moist eyes.

"Degu. I'm not able to see into your visions; only my own. But I saw you twitching and heard your cries." She continued to hold his hand in a soft embrace, her large hands nearly matching his own.

Degu's breathing stretched and slowed. He repeated himself. "How did you get here?"

"I followed you when you went after Rojo and that lady, I mean your grandmother. I saw you fall in the water, and I, I, well, I heard voices, or something. I'm not sure what it was. I mean, it sounded like you but it was muffled. You were talking to someone, or something. All I heard back was a garbled whine."

Degu thought about his encounter with Wohali in the womb. Ebony continued, interrupting his memory.

"I don't know why, but I dived in after you. I couldn't see you. I was afraid you were . . ."

Ebony looked away from Degu.

"How did you know the lady was my grandmother?"

Ebony's dark, liquid eyes returned to Degu's. "When I came up out of the water, I was blinded by a shaft of light. I shielded my eyes and turned away. When I did this, I saw my shadow. It, it separated itself from me somehow. I don't know how. But it rose from the ground and stood in front of me. And then it spoke to me, in my own voice, but lower in pitch. It told me where I was, here in the Ad, Adan, Adan—"

Ebony jutted her jaw forward, trying to complete the word.

"Adanvado," Degu offered.

"Adanvado," Ebony repeated. "It, I mean she, then told me you were led here by your grandmother and Rojo. My shadow said your work here was critical to restoring the balance in both worlds. She said that your visions would guide you, and that, although I cannot know your dreams, that I am here to be with you."

"Uh, um, okay. Okay. I guess I should tell you what has happened to me."

Degu swallowed, took in a gust of breath, and began to recount all of his experiences, beginning with the human-eyed bullfrog at the underground spring, and concluding with his dream of the massive oak tree being consumed by the ravenous, glowing bugs.

"And then, you appeared and pulled me out of the vision."

"I'm sorry Degu. I heard your screams. I panicked. I, I . . ."

"It's okay Ebony. I think my dream was over. But what does it mean?"

The pair stood in silence, still holding hands, searching each other's eyes for direction. Degu unconsciously began caressing Ebony's hand up and down with his thumb. He took instant comfort in her presence. Ebony broke the stare to look down at Degu's hand, at which point he became self-conscious and quickly pulled it back to his side.

"Um, maybe, if we go and find the tree, maybe we're supposed to, I mean, maybe I'm supposed to save it from the bugs. Although I don't know what that has to do with my grandmother, or Wohali." Degu's voice flattened and trailed away. He hadn't the first clue of how to proceed.

Ebony caught his slackening spirit and lifted him. "Hey, the horse! The horse was there by the tree in your vision. You said this was the same horse that changed into the old man running away with your grandmother."

"Yeah?"

"Well, if we find the horse, maybe we will find your grandmother. Maybe they will help us." She paused. "I wonder what the tree has to do with your brother though."

Degu scratched the back of his scalp and shrugged.

"Are you sure the other person with your grandmother wasn't Rojo? My shadow said you were led here by both of them."

Degu looked past Ebony toward the end of the field where it met the horizon. "I'm sure. This man was smaller and much older than Rojo."

"What, what do you think happened to him, to Rojo I mean?" Ebony asked.

Degu shifted his sight over to the edge of the forest. He was beginning to feel the exhaustion of speaking so many words, even with this new friend whom he already trusted. His eyes lowered. "I don't know."

Chapter 7

The pair sat silently in the circle of light; Degu continuing to stare at the ground; Ebony keeping vigil with her friend. Without looking up, Degu spoke. "I think the path I was walking on in my dream was in the other direction, away from where I last saw my grandmother and the man."

"What makes you think that?"

Degu shrugged. "I don't know. I just do . . . maybe."

Ebony reached out and touched Degu on the arm. "You decide, Degu. I trust you."

At these words, Degu cut his eyes up towards her. "Um. Uh." Degu wore his overwhelming fear like a second skin, with more of an endodermic quality to it. He was startled by the thought pushing forward in his mind. He finally released it and sighed. "Let's go find the path. I think my El-li-si will show up when she is supposed to. The same goes for Rojo."

He pressed his palms together and felt the sting from where his hand had been stabbed by the giant blackbird. He remembered the yo-yo. *The time has come. Wohali awaits. Find me, know Wohali.*

Degu stood and brushed the loose grass off of his pants. He noticed inside of the circle, the grass was fresh and green. He scrunched his eyebrows and looked over to the trees that still showed an abundance of freshly furled leaves and budded flowers awaiting their turn. He saw the turkey vulture sitting in the regal oak tree. He raised his arm timidly, pointing at the bird, at which point it lifted and thrust its wings. It swooped into the meadow and sailed in the direction Degu had suggested, maintaining a modest height and pace.

"Come on Ebony! We gotta follow that bird!" Degu grabbed her hands and pulled her up. The two then began running after the broad-winged guide. Soon the tree line paralleling the meadow gave way to a broader expanse. The pair were losing ground to the vulture who approached and then disappeared over a small hill. Degu and Ebony were both tiring. They slowed when they reached the base of the ridge. Sucking in air, together they took long, lumbering strides with their hands on their thighs. Summiting the hill, they stopped.

Before them lay another wide pasture replete with various grasses of brown, light green and orange-red hues. A rumble of brush pockmarked a landscape that was bisected by a meandering split rail fence made from small ash trees. Many miles in the distance, a mountain range rose abruptly. Degu was startled by the harsh look. The mountains were black with mottled bright yellows throughout.

"Do you see the vulture?" Degu asked through heaving breaths.

Ebony didn't answer, arms at her side, staring ahead.

Degu looked at her and then followed her sight line. She seemed to be looking out into the vacant field. "Um, Ebony? Do you see the vulture anywhere?"

"I, uh, no, no I don't"

Degu caught his breath and stood up straight. "What are you looking at?

Ebony pointed. "My shadow . . . and all of . . . the people."

Degu again looked at the vacant meadow. "I don't see anybody."

Ebony broke off her stare and turned towards Degu. "Do you mean . . . Am I the only . . . Uh, Degu, they're shadows too."

Degu measured his thoughts and words. "What do you mean, shadows?"

"They look like spirits, but something doesn't feel right. They're both dark and translucent. I don't see the Light in them. Their movements are heavy and diseased."

With these words, Degu stepped closer to Ebony. She was shivering and holding her hand up to her mouth. Degu tentatively put his arm around her waist and pulled her into a stilted embrace. She accepted his gesture while maintaining her frozen stare at the shadow masses.

When Degu released her, he turned and saw several vultures circling high and gliding along the edges of the left half of the meadow. He tried to imagine Ebony's vision. In doing so, he pictured the vultures serving as border collies guiding a large flock of shadowed sheep. The birds felt benevolent to him. They were steadfast in their jobs. Unlike the reputations of vultures back home, who were seen as filthy, ugly creatures that relished the fatal misfortunes of others, these beings exuded a spirit of motherly nurturance and fatherly patience.

Degu couldn't discern if any of these aerial custodians was the one that had spoken to him before. "Do you see the buzzards?"

"Yes," Ebony replied absently.

"Although I can't see the people, I mean the Shadows, I think the buzzards are helping them."

"I hope so. They look so sad; actually, they feel desperate to me."

"Do you think we should follow them?" Dego asked.

"Um, yeah I do."

Degu took a step toward the left side of the meadow when Ebony grabbed his arm.

"I think we're supposed to walk on the right side of the fence."

"Why?"

"Because my shadow is waving her arm and pointing us towards the right side."

"Where is your shadow?"

"She, um, she's over there," Ebony mumbled and nodded her head at the left side.

Degu saw her face drop. He redirected his steps, moving back over to the right side of the meadow. They walked along at a moderate pace. Several times Ebony stumbled over clumps of brush. Her eyes were fixed on the Shadow people. After the third occasion of nearly falling, Degu, reached over and grasped her hand. She turned to him and smiled. For all of the surreal things that had happened to him, in this precise moment, when he was holding her hand, Degu felt a surge of self-possession. He'd never experienced the sureness of having a purpose. As they walked on, while he thought about the admonitions from his grandmother, the bird-skull, and even the enigmatic yo-yo, in this time and space, he felt a certainty about being with Ebony. He now understood she had her own journey here. Yes, Degu was told he was on a quest to find his brother. He had many doubts about this journey. But Ebony was also here to right some wrong in her and her family's past. And he was to be here for her, just as much as she was to be here for him. He gripped her hand tighter.

They continued in silence. Ebony was now staring at the ground in front of her, still holding onto Degu's hand. They had been walking for what felt like several hours and were approaching the base of the mountain range as the sun was setting halfway behind the ridge top. For the first time, Degu noticed he was hungry, and the air felt a bit cool. He thought Ebony must be hungry as well. He started to worry again.

I don't know the first thing about finding food out in nature back home. What are we supposed to do in this *place? How am I going to take care of Ebony? What if it gets cold tonight? Are we safe out here?*

Just before dusk, Degu noticed a curling rope of yellow smoke. He followed its trail down to the chimney of a small dilapidated wood frame house perched on multiple sets of two cinder block columns, positioned along an open crawl space. The grey clapboards along the side were worn, bowed and splintering. The white tin roof had streaks of copper colored rust leading down to the front porch overhang, which was pitching forward. The roof was curled along the edges leaving the weathered trusses slightly exposed. *Clearly this place was abandoned long ago*, Degu thought.

Approaching the house, Degu saw that the front door was missing, along with the bottom half of the window in the frame to the left. The confidence he felt earlier eroded. "Um, Ebony? Something's not right about this place."

Ebony echoed his concern. "I know. It looks abandoned, but someone must be in there. There's a fire, and I can smell something cooking. I don't understand why there is a house in the Adanvado. I thought there wouldn't be any people here . . . I mean real . . . I mean, you know, living people."

She immediately scanned back over to where the Shadows were. She looked over to the split rail fence that ended at the entrance of the yard to this old house. Her eyes suggested she was tracking the Shadows. They darted to and fro in fits and starts. Eventually, her gaze settled directly in front of them as if some of the Shadows were frozen in place, facing the house.

Degu stood still, quickly receding into his former, passive self. Ebony noticed the growing vacancy in his eyes.

"Degu. We'll get through this. Degu, stay with me. I need you. We'll figure it out together. All of it." She paused and then added, "I'm really hungry, and it's getting cold now. What should we do?"

Ebony's question and vulnerable tone staunched Degu's slide and modestly renewed his sense of purpose. He still felt uneasy about entering the house. Underneath the smell of frying meat, there was an odor of deceit and malevolence. Degu crawled back to trusting his newly found instincts. He began to survey the surrounding area when a flurry erupted from inside the house.

Caaawwww! Caaawwww!

The two giant blackbirds shot out of the open door frame and sped away into the gathering night. In their wake, the turkey vulture tottered out onto the front porch. He slowly spread his enormous black wings, lifted, flapped twice and coasted into a landing in front of the couple.

"You're right to be cautious about entering this dwelling, Degu," the bird said. "But you need a few things from inside. My committee and I will watch over you. Just don't stay too long."

Degu nodded and took Ebony's hand. They stepped toward the house as the bird flew up and perched on the pitch of the roof, next to where the tin had curled and exposed the interior. He would stand sentinel while they were inside. Degu stepped first through the threshold. The smell met him with the force of a breaking ocean wave. He quickly jammed his mouth and nose into the crook of his left arm and scanned the perimeter of the darkened one room house. The only light sources were an oil lamp that sat alone in the middle of a dusty pine kitchen table, and the low flame emanating from the large brown brick fireplace on the opposite end of the room. Beneath the table, he could barely make out a large bulge. *A dead fawn?* he wondered. Clustered around the fireplace were loose stacks of split logs and kindling branches, three dented tin coffee cups and two straight back wooden chairs. The rattan weaving in the seat of one of the chairs was fraying and hanging loose on the underside. Hooked to a rod across the fireplace pit were the handles of a large black cast iron pot. It was empty.

Degu turned, leaned back outside and sucked in a deep breath. "Cover your nose when you come in," he said, reaching out to escort Ebony inside.

She took his hand, and covered her mouth with her other hand. Stepping into the room, Ebony's eyes gaped. "Degu, this place, uh, Degu, I don't know. I don't think I can—"

"I know," he said through the muffle of his arm. "We'll be quick. The buzzard said we need some things in here. I'm guessing one is some food. I don't know what else. There's not much in here. Let's see if we can find something to eat." He gestured toward the table. "I think that dead baby deer under the table is beginning to rot. It's killing my appetite. Maybe if I take it outside, it will smell better in here."

Degu moved haltingly over to the table while Ebony stood just inside the door frame. The form was indeed a dead deer. He hesitated, and then quickly bent over and collared the ankles of the animal, swinging it up and trotting over and outside with it. He tossed it with more force than he intended, sending it flying ten feet out in the front yard. It landed with a muted, lifeless thud. Degu then turned and walked back inside. The stench remained.

"My God, it's awful in here!" Ebony protested. Her face contorted as she walked over to the fireplace. She held her hands out to warm in front of the fire, then leaned over and peered at indistinguishable charred chunks in the pot. "How are we supposed to get the meat out of this thing? It's too hot to touch."

Ebony looked over at Degu who was exploring the dark edges of the room. "Why don't you use the lamp so you can see better?" she suggested.

"Oh. Yeah. Good idea," Degu answered, shuffling back towards the kitchen table. "Wait. What meat? There's nothing in the pot."

"Oh yes there is, although it so burnt, I can't tell what it is, or was."

"Huh. I must have missed that."

Picking up the lamp, the now portable light accentuated the banal feel of the space; stained walls of withering wood with splotchy green and black mildew reflecting down on jagged, rotting floorboards. Degu stood where he was. Given his height, he simply held the lamp up high, illuminating much of the room. He then did a slow, deliberate 360 degree scan. The room was barren, save for some type of aged parchment that was rolled up and leaning in the far corner by the fireplace.

Ebony moved over and stood by Degu. "The smell is worse over by the fireplace. Do you think it's coming from the meat?"

Degu squinted in the direction of the fireplace but still didn't see anything in the pot. He shrugged and returned to surveying the room.

Ebony continued. "There's really nothing in here. I mean, the vulture said there were things we needed in here. We know we need to eat, but what else? I mean, a dead baby deer. Old chairs and coffee cups. What are we supposed to do with those?"

Degu nodded in the direction of the parchment. "I think we need that."

Together they approached the scroll. Degu set down the lamp and gently picked up the old leather document. He laid it down by the lamp and unfurled it. It was a primitive map. There were clusters of disproportionate-sized mountains that looked like faceless noses, overlaid and protruding off the page. There was a trail marked by a curving series of X's. Three words in busy, untutored calligraphy anchored the trail, one at each end with the middle word being closer to the far left side. Placed between the two words closer to the end of the trail was a giant oak tree in the middle of a lake. Degu knew this was the tree in his dream. When he squinted to get a closer look at the words, Degu gasped and fell back.

Soaring   *Roots*   *Madness*

Degu sat stuttering, pointing at the words etched in brown stain on the scroll.

"What?!" From her crouched position, Ebony placed one hand on the open parchment on the floor. She looked at him with alarm. "What is it, Degu?"

"Those words. I, I wrote those exact words on my tree stand back home."

Ebony nodded slowly without further question or response, her look at the intersection of fear and wonder. She didn't break her fixed stare on Degu.

"I just wrote the word madness the other day. I, I, I was thinking about my grandmother."

Degu sat back up, trying to reclaim his composure while dusting off his hands. He coughed and gasped when another wave of stench rolled over them. He stuffed his mouth and nose back in the crook of his arm and breathed deeply. His voice was tremulous. "I'm going to roll this up. This map must be here for us. Maybe it will lead us to my grandmother and the horse."

Ebony nodded again and stood. "Maybe I can scoop some of the charred meat up with the coffee cups. I'll get a stick to use." She moved deliberately over and snapped off a short piece of kindling from the wood pile by the fireplace. As Degu rolled the scroll, Ebony reached carefully into the pot with the stick and cup.

"Aaaaaaaahhhh!!!"

Ebony dropped the cup and ran out of the house.

Degu's head jerked back and forth, trying to fix on whatever threat was in the room. "Ebony!" he yelled. Not seeing the threat, Degu hastily grabbed the roll and began to rush out of the house. He had only taken two strides when he landed awkwardly on a small, hard object he had not seen on the floor. His foot slid out from under him and he fell backwards, slamming his head on the plank floorboard.

Degu was awakened by a booming sonorous clap in the sky. He groggily lifted his head and tried to focus on his surroundings. He was lying on the ground outside of the house. It was now completely dark, except for a small, swinging light in the distance. The light grew larger as it moved in his direction. Suddenly a lingering, pulsating flash of lightning lit the sky, allowing him to clearly see Ebony running in his direction with an oil lamp and blanket.

"Degu! Are you okay?" She set the lamp next to him and opened the gray wool blanket to cover him. A powerful straight line wind pushed them both sideways and knocked over the lamp. Ebony righted herself and placed the light slightly behind her, using her body to buffer it from the wind.

"What happened?" he asked, still feeling slightly disoriented.

"Degu, it was the most horrible, the most evil . . . My God, I can't even . . ." Ebony stopped and took a deep breath. "Degu. You didn't see what was in the pot because . . ."

Degu propped up on one elbow while Ebony took in another breath. This time she spoke in a low monotone. "Because you can't see the Shadow people."

He looked away and stared into the dark, trying to comprehend what she was saying to him. He remembered the two black crows being chased out of the house by the buzzard. He recalled the smell of evil. He now understood that what he smelled was death. But not death that is within the natural order.

Ebony interrupted his thoughts. "I'm sorry Degu. I panicked when I touched one of the Shadow people in the pot."

Her shaking shoulders and voice betrayed that she was crying, although her face was darkened with the light at her back. Degu surprised himself by scrambling up and wrapping her with him in the blanket. He pulled her close, holding her tight in his arms. His mind went blank. He wanted to comfort her. "It's okay now," was all he could say.

After a few minutes, Ebony pulled back from Degu's embrace and exhaled through puffed cheeks. Her breathing leveled and she recounted the details of hearing Degu crash on the floor. She told him how, in spite of her fear, she had turned to go back into the house to check on him. It was then that two giant vultures swooped down out of the sky and joined the third that had been perched atop the roof. Ebony stopped, watching them dart inside. Moments later, two were dragging Degu out with sharp beaks clamped onto his shirt at the shoulders. The third followed with the parchment in his talons and, in his beak, a small object.

Degu gingerly touched the swollen knot on the back of his head and winced. "How long was I out?"

"Long enough for me to go search for food and shelter." Ebony then added meekly, "Actually, our people, um, my people, I mean the Shadow people, showed me where a lean-to is. It's just a little ways down the valley in that direction." Ebony motioned past the end of the fence line. "We need to get there before the rain starts and we lose the flame from the oil lamp."

Ebony started to throw the blanket off before Degu stopped her. He pulled the portion clinging to his back free and wrapped it around her. She paused and offered a wan smile. Degu was again captured in the beauty of those deep, obsidian eyes.

Another thunderclap broke the enchantment and the pair bolted in the direction of the shed. Minutes later, they arrived at the primitive structure. Degu was surprised that they beat the rain. He noticed how quickly the air had chilled, made colder by the strong, persistent wind shear. Degu rubbed his arms and blew into his hands to warm them. He noticed Ebony was shivering despite being wrapped in the blanket. He looked past Ebony and spied a large deer skin hanging in the back corner of the open room.

"You're gonna freeze in that thin blanket," he said.

Ebony's voice quivered through chattering clenched teeth. "What about you? You have nothing."

Degu stepped around her and lifted the large dried skin from the hook. He took one jagged corner and pulled it around his right shoulder and back. He then offered her the rest of the soft tawny pelt. His large hands clasped lightly onto her bony shoulders as he draped it around her. When she turned her head and caught his eyes, Degu glimpsed the reflection of the dancing lamp flame and the darkened silhouette of his face in the half moon pools of her eyes. He felt a warm blush spreading across his face. Ebony demurred and lowered her gaze.

Degu cleared his throat. "Um, the rain still hasn't started. Maybe we should try to eat something now." He slipped out of Ebony's embrace and raised the lamp and looked out into the night. The enormity of their situation washed over him. He thought that the prospect of finding any food now in the dark was highly improbable.

Ebony pulled the deer skin tighter around her. "It's okay, Degu," she sighed. "I don't think we're going to find anything tonight. Maybe we should just try to get some sleep."

He dropped his shoulders and the lamp to his side. He then thought back to the one room house and the empty pot in the fireplace. He tried to imagine what Ebony had seen. "Um, I'm sorry about the . . . I mean, what you saw."

Ebony lowered her eyes and looked to the side; her wound unmistakable. Degu then stepped to her and the two clumsily lowered themselves to the ground. He lied over on his side, leaving several feet of space between him and Ebony. She seemed to recover from the revisited image, spreading wide the edges of the deer skin in an inviting gesture. Degu hesitated and then scooched closer until he was lying prone beside her. Ebony smiled and wrapped her arm and the deerskin around him. She closed her eyes as Degu's spread into a wide stare. He held his arms stiff at his sides. Within a few minutes, Ebony was snoring.

Degu barely allowed himself to breathe. He had never known such a soft and kind embrace. He studied the contours of her face. Her skin had many scars and blemishes. To Degu, these were merely a part of her beautiful imperfection. He looked at her bulbous nose, high, broad cheekbones and thin, blanched lips and, for the first time, imagined a kiss. The image quickened his heart and breath. He felt a clamorous mix of arousal and peace. He closed his eyes.

I've never kissed anyone before. How wrong is it of me to kiss her now, while she's asleep? She's so beautiful. I don't know if, what should I, I can't help . . .

Degu quavered and drew in closer to meet her warm, moist lips with his own cool, chapped mouth. Instantly, he was transported to a meadow of the deepest green grass. The meadow abutted an endless field of corn, robust stalks standing ten feet high and heavy with hearty husks. He looked at Ebony, who lied beside him. She smiled dreamily.

Soon this peaceful image faded into a non-descript wall of beige and then black. The black then receded and the image of El-li-si came into focus. Degu sat up. It was morning and his grandmother was squatting over the dead fawn.

El-li-si!

He tried to orient to the situation. *I must have fallen asleep after I kissed Ebony.*

El-li-si looked at Degu and without betraying any emotion, turned and buried her face in the side of the corpse. She placed one foot on the animal's torso for leverage, and then, with her teeth clamped, tugged the hide upwards. She shook her head from side to side until the hide gave way, tearing in a long jagged line, revealing the deep blue muscle and thin, cloudy mucous membranes inside. She released the hide and dropped her face again into the inert flesh. Degu felt a wave of nausea. He rolled over onto his hands and knees and dry heaved. Because he hadn't eaten in quite a while, nothing came out.

When he looked up, the deer was gone and El-li-si was at a distance, standing next to a sapling. She was talking with the man Degu saw running away with her when he had first arrived in the Adanvado. Although he couldn't clearly see the young tree, he wondered if it was somehow connected to the oak from his first dream. Of course, it didn't reach to the heavens, but its *presence* was unmistakable. Degu still could not see the man's face. He watched in silence as the man handed a small object to El-li-si and then embraced her. He then stepped back. His boundaries blurred and darkened and he was erased backwards in a vacuous wind. El-li-si stood fixed in the same spot. Degu noticed a subtle stab of pain on her face. She turned towards him, smiled faintly, and moved off in the opposite direction from where the man had evaporated.

Degu scrambled to his feet and began to run after El-li-si, but she was gone in an instant. Wide-eyed, Degu scanned the expanse.

Nothing. Only the fields, split rail fence and abrupt rise of mountains surrounded him. He noticed a dull ache in his side that rolled across his abdomen. The ache reversed and rolled back, increasing in intensity. Through his confusion, he clutched his stomach.

I've got to find something to eat! he thought, bending at the waist. Turning back toward the lean-to, he began to search along the ground, as if he might discover something edible lying about.

Around the backside of the lean-to, Degu noticed a lichen-covered crabapple tree. Being that it was dark and stormy the night before, he and Ebony hadn't noticed it. Degu saw that there was only one cluster of three pinkish-red berries on the tree. He reached up and plucked the small hard fruit from a crusty, blackened branch. Just as he moved the fruit to his mouth, a screech pierced the air.

Caaawwww!

The two ravens reappeared. The lead bird shot like an arrow at Degu's hand, knocking the fruit free. The second one swooped low and caught the cluster before it hit the ground. The pair then spirited off into the horizon. Degu started to rage but doubled over, pushing in on the pain he was feeling in his gut. He listed forward and wedged into a small space in the tree where the trunk branched into two main limbs. He felt the branches squeeze and shake him about the shoulders.

What is this!? Is this tree some kind of monster? Degu groveled and fought to free himself when he heard a soft, feminine voice emanating from the tree. *Was the tree talking to him?* The voice became louder and more familiar.

"Degu! Degu, wake up!"

Ebony was leaning over Degu, tugging on his shoulders. He opened his eyes with a start and pushed up onto his elbows. Ebony pulled her hands back to her knees, still leaning over him.

"You were having another dream. I didn't want to disturb you, but you started to thrash around. I was afraid you might hurt yourself." She paused. "Did . . . did you see something that will help us find your brother and grandmother? And, uh, Rojo?"

Degu again stared into the deeply drawing pools of her eyes. *How much of it was a dream?* He remembered the kiss. *Did I kiss you? Please, let it be so.*

"Degu? Are you okay?"

"Um, yeah. I, uh, last night, did you feel a, uh, did we—"

"Degu, we need to leave this place. While you were still sleeping, I got up and looked around some more. That storm last night. Well, it never rained. I was sure we would have some rainwater to drink this morning. I came back and looked at the map. I think I understand where we are and the direction we are supposed to go in and . . ."

Ebony suddenly stopped and looked down.

Degu sensed the shift in Ebony. She seemed more resolute than when he first encountered her here in the Adanvado. He thought of the Shadow people and looked around then to the empty views. "Did you talk more with the, with them?"

Ebony didn't break her downward gaze.

"I think I'm here for another purpose. I mean, I believe, as my shadow told me, that I am here to help you find your brother, but I think that I am also supposed to lead them, I mean the Shadows, to another place; to home."

"Did they talk to you? I mean the others?"

Ebony started to speak but then paused. "We've got to eat something. We have a long journey ahead of us. We need our strength. And we've got to get going. There's no time to lose."

Degu looked out past Ebony and was surprised to catch sight of a lifeless form lying outside of the lean-to. Degu's mind flashed to the image of his grandmother eating the dead fawn. He then remembered the night before, back in Oak Ridge, when he thought he saw her eating the deer in the front yard. A sickening feeling began rising within his core.

"We have to eat that," he said pointing hesitantly. "Muh, maybe we can clean and dress it, and then cook it."

Ebony turned and saw the fawn. "Where did that . . .? Uh, that does seem to be all we have around here. Uh. Okay." She paused, looking back at Degu, "But there's no way to prepare it, and no time. Soooo . . ."

"What do you mean?" He gave her a stricken look. "We can't eat it raw?! We'd never, we'd get sick, we, I can't, Ebony."

"Degu, we need our strength. Already, I'm too weak to open it up. I don't like this any more than you do. Degu, please."

Degu shuddered, rose and lumbered toward the animal. He put his hands on its side. While the image of El-li-si burying her face in its flesh reappeared, he felt an almost imperceptible slit in the animal's pelt and followed it with his fingers. It ran most of the length of the fawn's breast. Degu forced himself to push his hands into the cut, feeling its cold, thick, wet muscles. He then jerked violently at the edges of the opening, exposing the deep blue and gray flesh within. A quick wave of nausea caught in his throat. Immediately, he thrust his face into the meat. His teeth slid over the mucous-covered surface a few times before he finally got some traction. He tore into the flesh and pulled his face up. With milky slime dripping on his face, he squinted and chewed hard and fast. The meat was tough. He felt another wave of nausea gurgling up. He swallowed the first bite in a successful attempt to push the nausea back down.

Degu felt something unexpected, something surprisingly natural even, in taking his food this way. His fear and disgust quickly dissolved as he leaned in and took another bite. This time however, he did not chew the chunk of flesh that he tore from the carcass. He gently spit it into his hand and reached over to Ebony. She winced and gagged, a tear forming from the corner of one eye.

"Please," Degu said. "Please try to eat. You're right. We have to have our strength. I don't know why, but I know this food is safe for us. Please eat."

He further extended his hand with the ragged meat towards his friend. Ebony reached her hand forward, hesitantly at first, before lunging, grabbing the piece and cramming it into her mouth. She grimaced and scrunched her eyes tight, pushing rhythmically down on the meat. Eventually she swallowed and then opened her eyes and gasped for air. A mix of oil and blood trickled down the side of her mouth.

Degu stood, watching her. Ebony took another deep breath.

"You're right, Degu. We were meant to, to have this."

With these words, Degu went back to tearing out chunks of flesh for the two of them to eat.

Having finished eating, Degu remembered the crabapple tree from his dream. He told Ebony, and walked around the side of the open shed to see if it actually existed. Rounding the back corner, he saw before him a shriveled, gnarled, blackened tree. It was impossible to determine what it was.

Ebony was close behind, calling out to him, "Degu, we really need to get—ahhhhh!!!"

Ebony grabbed his hand, turned and started pulling him away with her.

"GO, GO, RUN."

Degu knew instantly that Ebony saw something that he couldn't. He turned and sprinted away with her. He eventually settled into a long and gangly lope, and was able to keep pace with Ebony's more graceful, if not gritty, manner of running. Her face wore a horror unknown to Degu here in the Adanvado. His experience was confusing and, at times, deeply fretful, but he had yet to experience the demons that seemed to plague his friend. And yet, she possessed a confidence he knew he did not. Even when she was afraid, she was able to *respond* in the face of the fear.

When they had gotten about a hundred yards away, Degu remembered the map. He reached over and cupped her free swinging arm, slowing her to a stumbling trot. "We forgot the map," he said through staccato pants.

Ebony stopped and walked in a tight circle, one hand on her hip, the other lightly tapping on her sweat-laden forehead. "I, I, I, yes, you're right. We need the map."

She turned to Degu, panic spearing her eyes. "Degu, there were parts of the Shadows, they were, they looked like shreds of cloth hanging all over that tree. Degu, it was horrible. The moans. I heard them before I followed you around back. I thought they were coming from the house way back down from where we came. I didn't think . . . Degu, it was so awful."

She was shaking at this point.

Degu was trying to take in all that she was describing. *What happened to her confidence?* He felt compelled to pull her into an embrace, to comfort her. He stood still. His arms and shoulders felt like they were cloaked in a lead apron. His thoughts sped up.

"I, we can, I will go back with you to get the map."

Ebony looked down and shook her head.

"Are you alright?" Degu asked, putting his hand on her forearm.

She pulled it away. "I cannot go back there, Degu. You cannot ask me to do that!"

Startled, Degu stepped back. "Uh, okay. Okay. I'll do it. I'll go."

Degu began jogging, trying to visualize the Shadow people that Ebony had been seeing since they set forth on this journey. He pictured darkly translucent forms, taking the shapes of reflections in funhouse mirrors. He thought of what form the burned shadows took in the pot, only able to envision lifeless, molded clumps. Finally, he imagined shreds of dark, sheer fabric, caught in the cragged, deformed tree, blowing in the modest breeze.

Approaching the lean-to, he saw the leather parchment against the right inside wall. Peeking out from slightly behind the roll was a small, glossy brown object. Coming closer, Degu's eyebrows arched and his face opened. He rushed over and scooped up his childhood toy yo-yo, again dwarfing it in his big hand. He jerked his head up and to the side, searching for the giant ravens that had stolen it previously. While he held it, he started hearing a low pitch wailing coming from behind the shed. This startled him so that he dropped the yo-yo. Instantly, the sounds were silenced. Degu looked around, his heart racing and pupils expanding like bleeding ink stains. Delicately, he leaned over and corralled the toy in his long fingers. Right on cue, the moans returned. Degu sealed the yo-yo tight in his fist, grabbed the map and sprinted back towards Ebony.

Ebony stood, tightly wrapped in her own, long sinuous arms, bobbing almost imperceptibly on her toes. Degu came rumbling towards her.

"I heard them! I heard them, Ebony."

The map slipped out of his hand as he bent over to catch his breath. The yo-yo fell from his grip and bounced on the ground. While he reached down to retrieve it, Ebony opened her mouth to speak, but then said nothing.

"It was my yo-yo! I saw it behind the map. It—"

"That's what one of the buzzard's carried out of the evil house when they brought you and the map out!" Ebony blurted, pointing at the object that Degu had retrieved and now held in his opened palm.

That must have been what I slipped on running out of the house, Degu thought.

"How, how did you hear the, um, how, the people, you know, the Shadows?" Ebony asked.

"It's the yo-yo. When I held it, I heard, you know, the sounds."

Ebony paused and looked past Degu, to the surrounding grounds, as if tracking something or someone.

"Can, can you see them . . . now?" she asked.

Degu followed her sight line over his shoulder and stared into the empty expanse. His face dropped a bit. "No," he said over his shoulder, still looking out into the open space. "No, I can't."

Ebony stepped over to him and placed her hand on his shoulder. "They're still troubled. Watching them now, they're so restless and, disturbed. There's no peace here for them."

Degu stood with Ebony's word's ringing in his ears from earlier in the morning. He felt the smooth, round contours of the toy in his hand, and began to wonder how everything fit together. There was something mystical about this object. He remembered back to the sounds of his brother's name when he first played with it as a child. He thought of the ravens stealing it, and then the buzzards returning it to him. He knew now that this was necessary for him to find his brother. He tried to push the thought out of his mind. It must also be needed to help Ebony with the Shadows. He reluctantly began to think that their two journeys were meant to be one.

He looked up and saw Ebony had returned to holding herself in a tight embrace. Her agitation returning, Degu knew they had to get moving. "Let's look at the map again, to see where we're going." He then asked, "Will they follow us?"

Ebony nodded.

Unfurling the map, Degu pointed to the X's that curled around and up into the mountains. He noticed a small picture of a path just to the right of where the X's knifed into the crude scribbles representing the mountains. It was not there before. The path was covered in copper colored flakes, ascending into the mountains which were shrouded at their bases in a sage green and soft violet haze. Half way up, the mountains were covered in what looked to be snow, albeit a thick, dark gray version with pinkish undertones. Before Degu spoke, Ebony pointed at the image.

"What's that?"

Degu drew a deep breath and looked again at the word *Madness* etched just above the picture. He frowned.

"That's where we're going."

Ebony replied, "I thought we were already there."

Chapter 8

The beleaguered pair walked in silence for a while, each lost in their own thoughts. Degu shoved the yo-yo in his right front pants pocket so as not to be further troubled by its sounds. They reached the base of the path and saw the colorful cloud from the map sitting low over the trail. Degu turned to Ebony, who was staring over her shoulder. He surveyed the empty land behind her and then gently touched her on the arm.

"Are they following us?"

Ebony nodded without breaking her gaze.

"Are there any of them ahead of us?"

Ebony rotated and looked intently ahead. She shook her head this time.

"Do you think it's safe? I mean, why aren't some of them ahead us?"

Still, Ebony offered no audible response. She shrugged her shoulders and pulled in her bottom lip. She lowered her chin and drew closer to Degu. She was still struggling with the images she had witnessed earlier. Degu felt helpless to comfort her. He clumsily put one arm around her waist and began to move them toward the path. Nearing the cloud, he could see through it, to the long, slow climb that lay before them. He paused and looked down on the top of Ebony's head as she continued to hold tight to him. Degu took a deep breath and stepped with her into the brightly hued mist.

Nothing, he thought. *I don't feel anything different.* He released Ebony from their embrace while still holding firmly onto her hand. They waded through the haze for a few moments before stepping out into a clearing. The path up the mountain he had seen was gone, replaced by a snowy plane. Instantly, they were now at the summit of the mountain.

Degu scanned the scene before them. The open field was carpeted in the purest white. He had forgotten about the grayer illustration from the map. The bare trees that lined the field's edges were heavy laden with the snow. The boughs were all bent over as if in a permanent bow of respect. Along the far end of the field, a giant moon hung low in the sky. It was a mottled mix of flat and translucent whites and out of the right side sprang a pure milky white rainbow that seemed to arc down and touch the ground beyond the far end of the field.

Degu tensed to buffer himself against the chill he expected to feel. He quickly realized that it was not cold. It was, in fact, quite warm. He shook his head and turned to Ebony. "This place is beautiful. And so peaceful. How can this be Madness?"

Ebony was beginning to release from the tension she had been carrying since the day before. "I don't think it is Madness. I think it's Glorious," she answered, letting go of Degu's hand and skipping out several steps into the untrodden snow. She laughed, pirouetted and, with arms extended, fell backwards onto the cushioned ground. She immediately sprang up to a sitting position. With eyes opened wide, she grabbed handfuls of the white powder. "Degu! It's not snow!"

Degu loped over towards her. "What do you mean?" he asked, dropping to his knees, and scooping two handfuls himself.

"It's not wet, and it, it feels like, it's warm and, um, I'm not sure." Ebony hesitated.

Degu sensed something too. He concentrated on the feel of the white granules in his hands. *I can almost feel a pulsing, as if these things are alive!*

With increasing caution, he stood and offered his hand to Ebony. She began to frantically brush the loose grains that were clinging to her clothes. Degu watched passively. When she finished, she looked first at him, and then beyond and around him. Her eyes narrowed and her mouth pursed.

Degu followed her stare to see the wood line directly behind them. "Are the Shadows, did they come with us?"

Looking back to Ebony, he saw her slowly shaking her head. Degu could see the worry had returned to his friend's face. "Um, maybe they can't come here. Or maybe we have to, I don't know, maybe we have to do something here to help them," Degu said, reaching out and gently brushing a few stray white grains from Ebony's arm.

She nodded and looked expectantly at him.

"Well," he said, considering the open field and the unknown substance that covered it. "Maybe we can walk along the edge to get to the other side."

He unfurled the map and noticed another small picture that was not there previously. It showed the field and the woods beyond. He didn't know what to make of this animated parchment.

"Um, I think we can make it before it gets dark."

Ebony's response was mostly inaudible.

"Okay."

The two again walked in silence along the perimeter of the field. Degu strained to reconcile the breathtaking scene all around them with the discordant, low-gravity hum coming from the white granules. The more they walked, the more ominous the sound grew. The feel of Ebony's hand in his was a comforting anchor. Briefly, he wondered if she felt the same way. The burdened trees seemed to lift ever so slightly when they passed by. His thoughts shifted.

I wonder if they are greeting us, pleading for our help, or signaling for us to run away as fast as we can.

They continued, nearing the halfway point. The giant moon gradually set lower behind the tree line, so that it was only visible at the tip. The white rainbow was now out of view. Degu and Ebony looked up at the same time to see a raft of light gray clouds that had moved over the deep blue sky. Rather than the usual fluff and curvatures, these clouds had a number of distorted geometric shapes, defined by hard lines and angles. They saw one cloud that took the shape of a raven's beak. Trailing the beak was the shape of an arrow's shaft, complete with the fletchings at the tail end. A moment later, they saw a string of tiny balls being shot out of the beak and floating down toward the large field. The objects were so white they were almost blue.

The two stood motionless, beholding the radiance emanating from the falling spheres. On the way down, the objects danced like carefree children. Their beauty was hypnotizing. Lightly touching down, the balls maintained their shimmering auras, sitting atop the granules covering the field. Degu released Ebony's hand and raced over to where several had landed. He slowed, kneeled and gently slid his large hands underneath one. Lifting it to eye level, Degu was drawn even further into the enchanting glow. He laughed. Ebony caught up and knelt beside him. Despite her initial hesitance, she too was quickly bewitched by the glowing orb in Degu's hands.

As the two remained transfixed, the ball started to twitch and contort. The aura receded and the object grew larger. Degu dropped it and fell backwards. Ebony jumped to her feet. Degu scrambled to stand just as the ball morphed into a creature. The pair raised their arms instinctively to shield their faces. Squinting, they saw a grotesque hybrid that was part human, part animal. The being was marked by uneven deformities. The left half of its face was protruding and long, in the shape of a hippo. Spittle hung from its blue-gray, whiskered snout. The other half of the face was sunken, a shriveled old man, registering a primal fear in its one weathered brown eye. The rest of the body matched the old man's human form, with the exception of his right lower leg, which was the thick hairless stump of the hippo. The sight before him brought to mind the images of the first beings Degu encountered in the Adanvado. The creature began to speak but the hippo's gnarled groan and the old man's words created an undecipherable cacophony. Degu and Ebony could only hear and understand a pleading tone coming out of the din.

Almost simultaneously, the remaining orbs around them grew and contorted before popping into various deformed animal-human hybrids. There were beings that were part child, with fair hair and blue eyes, and part lizard, with sharp black spiny backs; a pink rough skinned mouse with a large human ear protruding out of its back; and several fat, balding men with frog legs and stray elephant tusks curving out of their sides.

The scene horrified Degu and Ebony. She grabbed his arm and pulled him backwards with her.

"Let's go!"

The pair darted to the edge of the field and then sprinted along the side towards the far end. Twice Degu jerked his head back to see what the creatures were doing. The first time was so reflexive that he was just determining whether or not they were being pursued. The second time, he maintained his look long enough to fix on the eyes of one of the beings. This one was a dog, a yellow lab with a human's eyes and forehead. He managed to see the pain and distress in its eyes. Degu came to a skidding halt. He realized the creatures were in trouble. Ebony had run a few steps further before stopping and returning, standing slightly behind Degu. The indiscernible groans and chatter grew louder.

"I think they need us, Ebony."

She winced. "What are we supposed to do? We can't understand what they are saying."

Degu began to step onto the field when the white granules flooded up and over each of the newly hatched creatures. The misshapen beings fell instantly silent as they dissolved under the white blanket.

Ebony lunged for Degu's arm and pulled him back to her. Her voice quivered. "Uh, what just happened?"

Degu stared at the field, once again placid and beautiful. But now he was filled with complete dread. He glanced down and saw where the blanket of granules ended inches away from their feet. He looked ahead in the direction of the opposite end of the field, beyond which was the moon and white rainbow, no longer visible behind the trees. There was a narrow patch of packed bare brown soil outlining the field.

"Dego. Dego! What do we do now?"

Degu pulled his garbled thoughts back together, straining to focus. Again he looked ahead. This time he saw the vulture guide, perched high atop the bended bow of a tree at the end of the field. Maintaining his eye on the bird, he clasped her hand.

"We have to keep moving forward, Ebony."

The two proceeded with great care, stepping deliberately on the narrow brown path. Degu mostly kept his gaze set on the vulture, who sat sober and alert in the drawing distance. Occasionally he would glance behind him to see Ebony as she tiptoed with her eyes focused on the ground before her. The sky was beginning to darken. Degu thought of the moon that had now completely receded behind the trees.

I thought the moon always rose into the night sky.

He now toggled his focus between the vulture and the path in front of him. He thought that maybe the white granule creatures might offer some residual light that would ironically keep him and Ebony safe. When he glanced over onto the field, he paused and expressed a heavy breath. Ebony bumped into him and then followed his gaze. They saw the white blanket rolling over into the purest black, a foreboding, undulating wave approaching them. She wrapped her arms around him from behind and buried her face in the middle of his back. Degu surprised himself with the calm and self-assurance he felt in that moment. He knew instinctively he and Ebony were safe. The black wave would only reach to the edges of the field and the last of the granules, inches from where they stood.

For Degu, the more pressing concern was that they were now in complete darkness. He closed his eyes and thought of the vulture guide. *Nothing.* He then thought of El-li-si. *Again, nothing.* His mind was as dark as the scene around him. While Ebony shivered and continued to hold him tightly, he reached up with his hands and covered hers as they clenched across his chest. He then dropped one arm to his side. In doing so, his hand bumped against the hard yo-yo in his pants pocket.

My yo-yo! I wonder if it . . . maybe it will help us! Degu rammed his hand in his pocket and pulled out the small toy. In complete darkness, he fumbled with the object, feeling for the string loop to place over his thick middle finger. Having successfully done so, he unspooled the toy. A chorus of wispy, vacuous voices rose, giving Degu a start. He jerked out of Ebony's grasp.

"Do you hear that?!" He couldn't see Ebony but felt her warm breath on his neck. He was aware that she pulled back slightly.

"Uh, no. But I. I think the Shadows are here now. I mean, I can't, of course I can't see them now. But I feel them Degu. Yes, they're here."

"I know," Degu answered. "I can hear them through my yo-yo. Can you hear this?"

"No. What are they saying?"

"I can't understand them. It's like they're singing or chanting. But I don't understand the language." He paused. "It does sound a little familiar though. I think it's Cherokee."

"Degu, listen closely and try to tell me what you hear. I know some Cherokee."

Degu looked down to where his hand and yo-yo were. In the pitch black, he rolled out the toy again. The voices returned. He strained to make out what they were singing. "Um. It, it sounds like 'ga-lu . . . ga-lu' . . . I can't really tell what the last sound is."

Ebony repeated the sounds under her breath.

"Ga-lu, ga-lu . . . Dego! Is it ga-lu-tsv?"

"That's it!" he said into the darkness in her direction.

"They're saying 'come'! They want us to follow them, Degu. Follow the sounds, Degu," Ebony instructed as she reached out, fumbling for his hand.

With one hand behind him, holding onto hers, Degu continued to flick the yo-yo up and down to hear the location of the Shadow chorus as they walked. They fell into a steady rhythm and within a few minutes they saw a light appear in the distance. Drawing nearer, they could see it was a campfire in a clearing at the edge of the field. Just along the periphery of the light, the vulture stood, so that only his face was visible. When they reached the light and the fire, Ebony released his hand and jogged over to warm herself. Degu moved over to the vulture.

"Hi," he said, standing awkwardly beside the giant bird.

The vulture stared into the fire.

"Um, look I don't know what to say," Degu continued. "Aren't you supposed to tell me something? Give me some kind of advice?" Degu looked toward the fire and then back to the taciturn creature. He felt himself getting agitated. "I mean, c'mon man. We could've been killed by those, those things out there! This is crazy!"

The bird finally broke his silence. "No. This is Madness. You know your purpose for being here in the Adanvado." The guide added, "Do not lose sight of this."

And with those words, the giant bird spread his wings and lifted off into the black night.

"Wait a minute! I need to know what's happening! How are we supposed to . . ."

Degu glared into the darkness, then scuffled back to where Ebony was standing close and warming by the fire. He stood next to her and stared into the dancing flames. Realizing that he still held the yo-yo in his hand, he absently removed the string from his finger and stuffed it back into his pocket.

"Um, Ebony. We should get some rest now. We've had a hard day and we don't know what tomorrow will be like. I think we'll be safe here by the fire."

Ebony broke her own fire-fixed stare and lowered her gaze. She nodded and slipped down, first to a sitting position, then over on her side with her head resting in the crux of her elbow.

Degu's eyes followed her down. He remained statue-like for a few moments, his thoughts flickering with the fire. Soon competing voices began warbling through his head.

The Guide: *You know your purpose for being here.*

Then Ebony's words: *I think I'm here for another purpose.*

El-li-si: *We weren't supposed to a done it this way.*

The groan from the yo-yo: *Wohali awaits. Find me, know Wohali.*

Degu squeezed his eyes shut and placed the flat of his hands against his temples. *I don't think I can do this.*

"Degu."

The voice was low and airy. Then again louder and deeper.

"Degu."

Degu was yanked from the noises in his head. He looked over at Ebony who was now holding him in a soft gaze.

"Will you come lie with me?" She asked with a faint smile that still betrayed some of the fear she had accrued over the past two days.

Degu nodded and folded down behind her. At first he kept his hands clenched against his chest, leaving a few inches of space between him and Ebony. Without looking over at him, she reached back and pulled his top arm over and around her midsection. Degu remained breathless for several seconds before his lungs surged open. With an expansive exhale, he released and molded more naturally into her back. Soon, both dropped into deep sleep.

Chapter 9

Degu sat up. It was morning. Ebony was in front of him, still sound asleep. A few wisps of whitish smoke curled upwards from the charred campfire embers. Degu shivered and realized he now felt chilled. Looking out beyond the small enclave where they were positioned at the edge of the field, he noticed that everything had returned to white. The meadow was a pristine blanket of freshly fallen snow. The texture appeared to be different. He sensed that this time it truly was snow. He noticed the trees, while still bowed under the weight of the snow, were more upright.

He recognized that his throat was parched. They had not had anything to drink since they arrived in the Adanvado and had not eaten since early the day before. *Maybe those things are gone now,* he thought. *Maybe I can gather up some of the real snow for me and Ebony. We've got to have some water and food. We'll figure out the food later, but for now, I'll see about the snow.*

He stumbled as he stood up. Wiping his hand across his dry lips and pallid face, Degu stepped towards the edge of the field and the snow line. The blue-white crystals glistened in the low morning sun, the reflection causing Degu to squint and shield his eyes. The snow *smelled* pure, pure and abrupt. Degu's belief in its healing properties grew. He jogged over and paused at the edge of the field. It didn't seem appropriate for him to despoil the virgin snow by trampling on it. He knelt on the bare ground by the edge and carefully swept his huge arms in a wide half circle, creating a mini mound of snow pulling into his chest. He realized he had nowhere to put the snow so he left the small pile and trotted back to where Ebony lay. Looking around, he saw nothing that would work as a container.

He thought about waking Ebony, but decided against it. She looked so peaceful. He remembered how frightened she was the day before. *It's good that she can sleep. She needs the safety of her sleep to help her regain her strength.* Degu stood for a few moments staring. He noticed that her eyes were sunken rather deeply, almost as if they were holes in her large oval head. He sensed that many would not look upon her as classically beautiful, and this puzzled him. With each suspended moment that Degu gazed at Ebony, he drew further and further into the seamless, hypnotic feel of her comeliness. He felt renewed in her grace. His belief that he would be with her and care for and protect her surged up into his shoulders.

Degu decided to wander a ways into the woods beyond the field and the enclave where they camped. He would search for both food and some type of container to hold the water from the melted snow. He found a thin meandering trail through the tall, erect pine trees that stood in an irregular pattern. Interspersed among the pines were random birch and cedar trees. Soon he noticed another clearing ahead. He paused and looked back, trying to register the path he had traveled so that he could find his way back to Ebony. When he turned back toward the clearing, he saw a figure. He was sure it was not there the moment before. Narrowing his eyes, he stepped forward. The figure had its back facing Degu. As he silently moved ahead, the size and shape became familiar; the humped, drawn in shoulders, the bald head.

"Grandma?!" Degu began to jog forward.

The figure did not move. "El-li-si!"

Degu was now in a full sprint. Still the figure did not move. Approaching the being and reaching out to touch its shoulder, he called once more between pants.

"El-li-si?"

She turned and faced him. Her smile was slight, her eyes offering a hint of trouble. Degu froze. With his arm extended, he took in his grandmother's face. Despite the underlying weariness, he could see her love for him rounding out the worry lines beside her deep, black eyes. Her eyes shone as she drank in the sight of her Degotoga. He lowered his arm back to his side and stood grinning. He was flush with a sense of delight and relief at finding her.

"El-li-si. I'm so, so, I didn't know that I would find you. Are you okay?" Degu's mind raced with images of his grandmother from the past two days. He again reached out to touch her. As he did, she reached up with the palm of her hand, giving gentle rejection to his impulse to touch her. He smiled uncertainly and twitched. "I'm just, I'm, I wanted you to . . ."

El-li-si's smile rose and fell like one last tide receding out into the sea. "Degotoga, it's not safe to touch me just yet."

Degu was startled by the resonating tone and the contents of his grandmother's words. He had never heard her speak so clearly.

"But I don't understand," he said softly.

"Listen to me Degotoga. You don't have much time. The Adanvado is drying up. The Spirit World is dying. The balance between the Adanvado and the material world has been severely altered. This has allowed the Raven Mocker to become stronger and more concentrated in his spread of evil. The land is drying and dying. The Great Oak must be saved. You must find your *Wohali*. Only then will the balance be restored. I cannot do this for you. I cannot come with you yet."

"But, but, why not? What's going on El-li-si?" He remembered hearing the bird skull creature talk about this evil being. "Who, what is the Raven Mocker?"

El-li-si seemed to ignore his questions, turning and looking askance into the forest canopy. "I sat with the Loblolly Pine and the

Mountain Pine Beetle yesterday," El-li-si mused. "These two creatures used to live in Balance. You might look at the Pine Beetle and think, 'this bug destroys the tree. What good comes from this?'"

Degu nodded as his grandmother continued.

"In Balance, the Pine Beetle clan only takes enough to feed their families. The Mother Beetle understands that if they take too much, they will overpopulate and need more and more Pines to eat. She knows that they will number far too many for the Woodpecker Clan to feed upon. Eventually, there will be no more left in the Pine family, and then Mother Beetle's family will starve, and the Woodpecker Clan will follow. When her clan eats the right portion, both the Beetle and Pine clans remain healthy, the forest nourishes itself, and Life is sustained. We are all from the same family, Degotoga. The trees are your brothers. We all have the same Mother."

"I think, because of Ebony, I think I'm starting to understand what you are saying, El-li-si."

El-li-si smiled and continued. "Yesterday, both the Beetle and the Pine told me of their alarm of the changes in the Adanvado. The Pine Beetle's cousin, the Oak Bark Beetle, has been possessed by the Raven Mocker. They have consumed the Oak clan at an unprecedented speed. Among all of the tree clans, the Oaks were leaders. With their stout trunks and high reach, they breathed strong breaths into the sky to help stir the clouds. The Loblolly told me that he no longer can see his cousin the Oak. The word has spread through the forests that the Oak Clan may be lost. We are no longer receiving the rains that quench all of the clans. Our only chance is to hope that the Great Oak still survives. This is *my* quest; to find and protect the Great Oak."

Degu swallowed and sucked in a breath. The image of his first dream in the Adanvado was florid in his mind. He saw again the rush of creatures and the tsunamic speed with which they devoured the tree. He now understood that this was the Great Oak being destroyed by the Raven Mocker's Bark Beetles. His eyes grew larger.

"But, so, I don't see how this involves me . . . and my . . . Wohali."

Staring at him, El-li-si spoke plaintively. "I cannot know your visions, Son; only my own. But I have something important to tell you. Just before your grandfather died, he told me of his last vision. He said that I must give you—"

THUD.

Without any notice of sight or sound, a large pine tree fell, glancing Degu's side and knocking him to the ground. El-li-si was directly in its path. Degu shot up and began frantically looking for his grandmother beneath the behemoth trunk. She had vanished. Degu screamed and clawed at the ground.

"El-li-si! Grandma!"

While he dug under the tree, a black shadow trailed up and away on the other side. Where the base of the trunk had shredded, a frenzy of black and crimson colored bugs scurried about.

"Dego, wake up! Dego! Dego!"

Degu writhed and swung his arm, connecting the back of his hand with Ebony's cheek. She fell to the side and cradled her jaw, wincing in pain. Degu bolted up, his heart pounding like a stone pulverizer in his chest.

"What? Ah, uh!" He leaned over to her. "What happened?! Are you okay? Who hit you?"

"You did!"

Still cringing and holding her jaw, Ebony reached out with her other hand to calm Degu. "I'll be alright. You were having a nightmare."

Degu shifted back and shook his head. "It was so real. Ebony, I thought I . . ." his words caught in his throat. He cleared his throat and spoke plaintively. "I thought I found El-li-si."

He continued telling Ebony about his dream. When he finished, his placed both dirty hands over his face, and pushed a heavy breath through his fingers. His nails were thick with red clay and trickles of blood from where he was digging at the ground in his sleep.

Ebony scooched over closer to his side and draped her arm around him. "It's okay. I mean, no, it's not okay, but we're here together, Degu. I guess I'm learning that visions can be really hard. Most of us don't even have them. I mean, I guess we don't. I see the Shadows and even talked with mine, but I don't get dreams."

Ebony repositioned herself in front of Degu. She caught his eyes in hers. "Degu. I trust you. We are supposed to do this together. I believe that my quest to help the Shadows and your quest to find your brother are somehow one in the same."

She paused to swallow and cough. Degu remembered that they needed water and thought of the new snow. He hurried to his feet. "I think the things from last night are gone. There's new snow. We can get the water from it."

He shuffled in the direction of the field which had indeed returned to its white, Eden-like form. Ebony's face flashed with alarm.

"NO! Degu wait!"

With his hands extending, inches away from the fair powdery cover, the sheen melted in an uneven small oval near him, showing a black and red pulsing mass. Degu lurched backwards. He turned and grabbed Ebony's hand and they sprinted into the forest, moving away from the field of Madness. On the ground near the soft mound of white and black flecked campfire ashes, lay the curled map.

Chapter 10

"Degu, I can't keep up."

Ebony heaved and sucked in air as she stopped and stooped over with her hands on her knees. They had followed a path through giant spindly aspen trees away from the field. The chalky white trees had irregular bark patterns with black etchings in the shapes of birds in flight. If not for the open space between the trees, the trail would have been barely noticeable, almost as if it were not trodden at all.

Degu, also winded, clasped his hands on his waist, tossed his head back and drew air in through his gaping mouth. He wiped the beaded sweat from his forehead, leaving a brownish smear. He noticed that the unique character of the trees was in stark contrast to the pines, birches and cedars of his latest dream. Degu shuddered, feeling the push of air as he relived the felling of the giant pine that pinned his grandmother.

"Ebony, what are we gonna do?"

Ebony had turned her back to him and didn't respond. She stepped, trance-like, off of the narrow path and into the foot high grass. The sun was now higher in the sky. Degu stood vacantly and watched while Ebony moved over to one of the trees. She reached out to feel the inviting white curls of bark that gave birth to the black images on the trees. She titled her head and reached out to caress one. Not looking back, her voice cracked as she called out, "Degu, come see this."

Dutifully moving toward her, he was curious and a bit confused. When he stood next to her, she pulled her hand away from the tree. There were several translucent orange drops on the tips of her fingers. "Do you know what this is?" Ebony asked.

Degu shook his head.

Bringing her fingers close to her nose, Ebony breathed in the saps scent. She closed her eyes and smiled. "Degu, it's soooo sweet." She opened her eyes wide and lifted her hand up to his nose. He leaned slightly forward to follow her lead. He sniffed twice and then scrunched his upper lip and nose in a rough circular motion.

"The smell kinda tickles me," he said, relaxing his face and smiling.

Ebony stared into the distance to the side of Degu and then dropped her smile. "Degu, do you think it's safe? I mean to eat this?"

"I don't know," he replied.

At the mention of eating, Degu felt the pangs of his empty stomach and the dry grit in his parched throat. He realized that Ebony must be feeling the same thing. Given all that they had experienced in this land of Madness, he thought that they should be careful. He gave a quick look around to see if there were any other credible food and water sources. They were deep into the aspen forest at this point. The trail meandered around a slight bend in the tree line, but all Degu could see was row upon staggered row of gangly white trees with varied black etchings. *What other choice do we have?* he thought peering back at the drops that crawled down Ebony's fingertips. The ether-like effect of the aroma made him bolder.

"Maybe I should try it first, to make sure it's not bad," he said.

She frowned. "What if it is? What if something happens to you? Degu, I don't think I can make it without you." She paused and stared at him. "I need you," she said, taking one hand and placing it on his side.

Degu was again swimming in the inviting black pools of Ebony's eyes. "Uh, um, well, we've got to have something to eat and drink. There's really nothing else around here." Degu then heard the dream echo of El-li-si's voice, talking about the trees.

The trees are your brothers.

"Ebony, it's okay. These trees are alive. They're not dying from this honey. It's their blood. It sustains them. I think they're offering it to you and me. They know we need nourishment to continue our quests, I mean our quest."

Ebony lifted her free hand containing the sap drops back to her nose and breathed in the ambrosia. She giggled. "That's funny. You sound all Native American, talking that way." She paused and then brought her fingers up to Degu's mouth. First with a hint of tease, she extended her index finger near to the tip of his tongue before quickly pulling it away and laughing. Degu raised his eyebrows and smiled. Then, almost delicately, she moved her finger back in, reaching into his open mouth and placing the drop in the middle of his tongue and slowly drawing it forward to wipe her finger clean.

Degu's eyes drifted inward as he focused on the taste. It was the purest nectar. He had never experienced something so rich, and yet light, so powerful, yet soft. A surge of liquid warmth rose in Degu's chest. His heart's pace quickened. He stared at Ebony and realized in that very moment, that he was going to kiss her. Mechanically leaning in, he moved close enough to feel the warm moisture of her breath when the quick creak and crack sounded in the near distance. Degu caught sight of the falling tree just as it was about to hit them. He shoved Ebony backwards as the tree sliced between them and crashed at their feet.

Degu jumped over the aspen and crouched by Ebony who wretched on her back. "Are you okay?!"

She rolled onto her side and labored to catch her breath. Degu's eyes darted back and forth. "I'm, I'm sorry. I didn't mean to push you so hard. I just heard the tree . . . I just saw it coming, I, I just, my El-li-si

. . . I'm sorry, Ebony."

Ebony continued lying on her side. She held her hand up to Degu to touch him and say that she would be okay. Within a few moments her breathing became more level. Degu's surge subsided but he never took his expectant eyes off of her. He was poised to respond to anything she requested. At last she sat up and brushed the dry grass and dirt from her clothes. When she did this, Degu relaxed more.

"I'm okay, Degu," she said curtly. In the silent space that followed, the pair heard a gurgling. "What's that sound?" she asked.

"It sounds like water!" Degu replied with a start. "C'mon. Let's go see!"

Degu pulled Ebony up with him and the two scuttled over to the sounds at the base of the fallen tree. Before them was an underground spring, similar to the one through which they had entered the Spirit World. Seeing the water only served to accentuate Degu's thirst. He didn't notice one major difference being the slightly burned white and brown foam lolling at the edges of the water. He stabbed his hand into the spring and scooped the warm amber colored liquid into his mouth. He tasted salt and butter which made him cough, smack his lips and cluck his tongue with the residue.

He noticed his hand began to feel tight and swollen. When he looked down, it was blurry. He felt light-headed and hot. Next, his head felt sodden and heavy. He labored to lift his chin and look over at Ebony. She looked angry. As he looked at her, Degu was aware that he'd never seen this expression from her. With her stormy eyes fixed beneath sharp angled brows and her jaw line jutting forward, she appeared almost baleful. Rather than feeling threatened, Degu was curious as time and sound seemed to slow. He watched her mouth move with distorted echoes, deep and slurry.

Suddenly she stopped. Everything stopped. Degu watched as a series of still frame pictures shuffled in front of his eyes. Ebony's mouth opened, her jaw unhinged and a torrent of oak bark beetles projected out of her throat. They pulsed and glowed deep red. In the final picture, the bugs burst forward and swarmed over Degu. Before blacking out, Degu felt the sharp stings of the bites all over his body.

The next moment, everything cleared. Degu's hand and head felt normal. There was no evidence of the welts he expected to see all over his body. He breathed in deep through his nostrils and glanced over at Ebony. She had gotten up and walked back to where she had found the sap. He watched as she hungrily lapped at the bark with a large black, rasp-like tongue that ripped off pieces of the bark as she went. Degu got up and jogged over next to her.

"Ebony, are you okay?" he asked, marveling at the fierceness of her task. Holding fast to the tree, without breaking her pace, she gurgled, "uh-huh". Degu hesitated and then looked over to an adjacent tree. He saw the clear orange substance oozing out of the open bark curls. Stepping over, he reached out and scraped a globule onto his finger. First he brought it back to his nose. Again, it gave him a lift and a tickle. He smiled, remembering its unique palate and then licked his finger. Once more, the taste exploded in his mouth. This time he noticed the competing swirl of warmth and coolness as the liquid dispersed over his tongue. He threw his head back and laughed before hugging the tree and ferociously licking the bark.

When he paused to catch his breath, Degu noticed the once still and vacant forest was now teeming with animal life. All manner of beasts were scattered throughout, each partnered with a single aspen tree; each licking the bark with equal ardor. He saw a mountain lion, shoulder muscles rippling, next to a sheep that was utterly at ease; a young brown elk back to back with a timber wolf; even a large ball python was shimmering its forked tongue against a tree, directly next to a small gray mouse. Degu stood, absorbing the grand sight before him.

He noticed a gentle hand sliding into his, grasping tight around his knuckles. Ebony angled around in front of him. She cupped her left hand around the back of his neck. This time, there would be no interference. She leaned up and pulled him down to meet her inviting lips. At first, Degu was surprised and mildly resistant. He then realized how soft and warm her kiss and caresses were, and he relaxed, kissing her more deeply. They ended the kiss with a couple of quick pecks. Degu smiled, realizing that he was holding her in a tight embrace. She felt so good in his arms. Given his struggles back home, Degu could never imagine himself doing this with a girl. In that moment, the enormity of the whole experience in the Adanvado was reduced and redacted. No matter what else happened, no matter if he found Wo-ha-li, if his El-li-si found and saved the Great Oak; if Ebony led her Shadow people to wherever they were to go; none of this now mattered as much as Degu being with Ebony. She was his spirit-mate. He was convinced of this. Maybe the quest was over. Maybe the other pieces were just stories and myths meant to get he and Ebony to this forest of Eden. Everything was perfect here. Everything was in beautiful harmony. The animals lived peaceably side by side. The trees offered unending nourishment. Maybe the balance that his grandmother spoke of had been restored.

Lazing in the deep black pools of Ebony's eyes, Degu was distracted when a flurry of movement crossed his peripheral vision. He looked up and saw the vultures banging into the aspens about 10 feet off of the ground. This action caused the other animals to stop feeding. With the disruption, the creatures turned towards each other. Degu could see the change in the animals' eyes; the predators' narrowed slits along with a slight crouch in posture while the preys' pupils widely dilated, accompanying their abrupt tensing. The predators pounced in unison and the volume quickly ascended as the previously peaceful land erupted in piercing squeals, groans and gasps.

Degu sprang up, opening his eyes. Everything was gone. The carnal screams were vanquished. All Degu heard as he scanned the now empty forest was his own hard panting and thumping heart. The animals were no more. Everything was as it was before he drank from the underground spring. He turned and saw Ebony sitting with her back against one of the aspens, her face buried in her boney fingers. She was crying.

"Ebony?" Degu whispered, before clearing his throat and calling more clearly, "Ebony? Are you okay?" He got up and moved over next to her.

Ebony wiped the tears away, then cut her eyes over to Degu. "I thought you were going to die."

Degu was confused. "What do you mean? Wha, what happened?"

Ebony tightened her face. "How could you do something so stupid? Didn't you see the color of the water, the oily sheen on the surface? Couldn't you smell it? Degu, it was poison."

Her words stung Degu. He fast-forwarded through all of the images that followed him drinking the spring water: Ebony's angry look and the bugs streaming out of her mouth and covering him; the kiss and embrace; the animals; the vultures and then the carnage. He shuddered. Once more, he was unsure of what was real. His head felt heavy.

"I'm sorry, Ebony."

She had a distant look.

"Can you tell me what happened?" he asked again.

"What do you mean, 'what happened'? You ran over and scooped up water, drank it, started gagging, passed out and starting convulsing! What little hair you had left fell out. Your face turned bright red. Finally you stopped and became very still. Degu, you scared me! I didn't know what to do. I looked around for the Shadows, for my shadow. Nothing. No one. I've been all alone here. How could you do this to me, Degu?!"

Degu sat back against the tree next to her. In his stupor, he reflexively reached up to feel his bald head. He was struck by how rough his skin felt. He angled his head to see Ebony. She was now sobbing. His heart sank.

"I'm sorry, Ebony."

She lunged over and grabbed him, burying her face in his chest. She hacked and coughed. Degu felt awkward and shaky. He finally reached around her with one arm and lightly patted her back.

She pushed back off of his chest. Her eyes were swollen. "Degu, we've got to get out of here. I think everything here is bad. After you passed out, I thought about eating some of the sap. I knew I would need more strength if you, I mean, I needed to eat. But when I got close to the sap and smelled it, well, at first it made me laugh. But then I stopped and realized that this was all wrong. I was so upset one moment and then giggling and feeling all happy the next. I realized there was something bad about the sap. I don't know why, but I decided to spit on it. When I did, it started steaming up. Eventually it was gone. For a few minutes, I spit on every tree around me. The steam was sizzling and rising up in a big yellow cloud. Eventually, I was too dry. I couldn't spit anymore."

Degu looked around and saw the trees that Ebony had spit on. Their bark was now whole, with no black etchings and oozing orange pus. He realized that he could have died from the sap and the toxic spring water. He wondered why he didn't. He slowly pulled in a long, deep breath. "You're right Ebony. We've got to get out of here."

The pair stood up and looked around. The barely perceptible path was now gone. "Which way should we go, Degu?" Ebony slipped her hand back into his, and offered a look seeking his reassurance and direction. Degu felt his frustration begin to rise. He was still trying to absorb his vision and near-death experience. He felt responsible for having led them into this poisonous forest and now he had no sense of how to get them out. His head began to throb.

"I don't know," he grumbled.

Ebony gripped his hand tighter. "C'mon Degu. You gotta figure this out."

For the first time, Degu felt agitation towards Ebony rising within his chest. "Why do I have to figure everything out?" he blurted.

Ebony's mouth opened as she released her fingers from his grip and turned to face him. "I didn't say you had to figure everything out."

"Actually, you just did, Ebony."

"I didn't mean . . . well, *you* were the one that got us in here."

Degu's anger now spiked. "All I have tried to do is take care of you since we've been here."

"Take care of *me*?! You patronizing jerk!"

Degu shot back. "Who tried the tree sap in case it was bad? Which it was. Who guided you through the darkness along the edge of the field with those, those evil things? Who was going to get you water from the snow? Or at least what I thought was snow. Who showed you how to eat the deer? Who went back to get the map when you were afraid?"

The map! he thought. Degu's demeanor softened. "Ebony, that's it! The map will show us how to get out of here!"

Ebony was smarting from his comments and didn't brighten at this revelation.

"C'mon Ebony! I'm sorry I snapped at you. We're gonna be okay. Let's look at the map. Remember, it showed the path through Madness over to the land of Roots and Soaring. Let's see what it says."

Degu patted his back pockets and began searching around for the map. He looked over expectantly at Ebony who was standing with her arms crossed. The look of hurt on her face was now replaced with one of smoldering ire. Degu stopped his search.

"I admit that I have been afraid, Degu. I have leaned on you to help me. But don't you dare make me out to be a helpless child. I'm the one who found us the shelter when you were knocked out on the floor in the cabin. I'm the one who stopped you from touching those creatures back by the campfire this morning. I'm the one who can see and talk with the Shadows. I'm the one who retraced our steps to find the map when you were *again* passed out, this time from the poisoned water." She glared at him. "I'm the one with a bruised cheek and sore ribs from where you hit me and pushed me down."

Degu's cheeks flushed. "Ebony, you know I didn't mean to . . ."

The two stood silent for a moment. "Um, I'm sorry, Ebony. You're right. I've not been very much help. Um, so, so do you, do you have the map?"

Ebony's look of hurt now rejoined the anger. "No. I found my way all the way back to the campfire. It's nowhere to be found."

They stood in lingering silence.

Finally, Degu shrugged. "I don't know what to say Ebony. Did you see the Shadows anywhere? I mean, they should be going the right way, right?"

"Don't you listen to me? I already told you, I don't see them anywhere!" she barked. "Why did you bring me here? The Shadows

102

didn't come here. We should've just followed them."

Degu mumbled his reply. "I thought they did."

"Some of them followed us in to this God-forsaken land. But they're not here now, are they? They're not in these evil woods that you drug me into."

"I did not drag you into here, Ebony."

"Actually, you did, Degu."

Degu raised his hands in exasperation and then brought them back down, slapping his thighs. Doing so, he felt the small hard lump of the yo-yo in his pocket. "Ebony, the yo-yo! Maybe we can hear the Shadows again!" He fumbled in his pocket and pulled out the slick veneer toy. Ebony brightened as Degu clumsily worked to slide it on his finger. He was having trouble with the knotted string when the sound pierced the empty woods.

Caaawwww! Caaawwww!

Degu and Ebony both jerked their necks upward. The two oversized ravens strafed low overhead, before making a wide swing and turning to come back at the pair. Degu hastened to get the yo-yo on his finger but dropped it on ground. It rolled several feet away. He glanced at the ravens and then dove at the yo-yo. The blackbirds zeroed in; one aiming for Degu's hand; the other going for the toy. Degu beat them by a split second, grabbing the yo-yo in his oversized mitt. Just as before, the one raven's beak then stabbed the back of his hand causing him to spasm in pain. The yo-yo dribbled free and was scooped up by the second bird, who proceeded to fly over and drop it into the poisoned spring water cauldron at the base of the fallen tree. Degu and Ebony looked on in horror as the yo-yo sank. The birds shot off, up and through the trees, leaving a trail of short cackles, the sound of mocking laughter fading as they disappeared.

"Degu!?" Ebony's plaintive cry pierced him once more. She collapsed to the ground, covered her face and sobbed.

Degu held his position several steps away from her, unsure of how to comfort her. He finally stepped forward, kneeled and began awkwardly rubbing her back. He watched her sobs slowly subside. He realized that she had fallen asleep.

Back home Degu never felt like he measured up to anyone's standards. In school, with his alopecia he knew that he was a freak show for the other kids. Because of his size, in the parks and on the playgrounds, the others expected him to be a great athlete, maybe in football or basketball, but he was clumsy and slow. At home, his parents were so busy doing what they wanted, he seldom felt like they even noticed he was around. This was his whole life, his whole bleak existence. That is, until recently. He met a new friend in Rojo, and then, finally, he met a beautiful girl. Ebony seemed like such a perfect match for him. It was fitting in Degu's cruel reality that his El-li-si would show up at school, *minutes* after he meets Ebony, and start the scene that set all of these events in motion.

Now, here I am, exhausted, sick and lost in this wasteland. I've hurt the only girl I've ever loved. I've lost my grandmother and best friend. I've got a monster twin brother that I'm supposed to find and rescue. Degu's thoughts stopped briefly while he gazed upon her still form huddled on the ground. *I only create problems for other people.* Water began to well in his lower eye lids. *She's really smart. She'll figure her way back to the Shadows. They'll find each other, I'm sure. I'll only get in her way. I'll only cause her more pain.* Degu felt a stab in his chest with this last thought. He looked on her one last time and then turned and walked away.

Chapter 11

Degu wandered aimlessly through the aspen forest, barely lifting his eyes enough to avoid banging into the trees. He had walked for what he was sure was a couple of hours. Given the leaf canopy above, the sunlight was largely filtered out; only occasional dust-filled rays broke through. The sharp pangs in his empty stomach had finally pitched and receded, so that now there was only a dense ache. His throat and mouth felt like paste. His thoughts dulled, his vision warbled. He stopped to rest and catch his dry breath. As he tried to swallow, his thoughts returned to Ebony.

"It was wrong for me to leave Ebony. I've really screwed up this time. I have to go back and make things right," he said aloud. He stood to go back and saw a burst of sunlight. He squinted, trying to focus. *What is that? Is that a clearing?* He looked around and could see that the forest seemed to go on endlessly. But this was definitely something different, something inviting.

"Maybe there'll be food and water! I can get some for me and Ebony." He quickened his pace in the direction of the light. Approaching the open space, Degu squinted even more, not having seen so much light for almost a full day. He walked into the clearing and the searing white light. He raised his arm and shielded his eyes in the crook of his elbow. He stood along the edge of the opening, and cast his sight to the ground. It was bathed in a milky white aura.

Degu knew he needed something to cut the strength of the light, something to shade his eyes. He lumbered around the edge of the tree line and came upon a plant with sheer red heart-shaped leaves. *These are perfect!* he mused, reaching down and pulling off two of the smaller leaves. Immediately, the broken stems withered and retreated into the ground. At first Degu considered holding the leaves in front of his eyes to use as sunglasses. He then stopped, carefully closed his eyes, and gently pressed and patted the leaves over them like a poultice meant to ease his tired and aching head.

The warm feeling slowly gathered, tingling his face. Then came the contrasting cool swirl. It heightened his senses, causing him to draw in a deep cleansing breath. He felt the leaves dissolve into his skin. Without thinking, he opened his eyes wide. The penetrating white light was still there, but it didn't blind Degu. In fact, he could see everything clearly through a light red tint.

The white rainbow! This is it!

Degu shot his look up to the sky. He followed the gentle arch that rose from this base all the way up to the moon. The moon was like a giant, clear globe with a light brown dusting on its surface. Degu saw a menagerie of animals and various plants and trees on the inside. Everything moved in perfect rhythm; there was an ease and flow that characterized the interactions of all sentient beings inside. Degu felt lighter. He noticed that the dull ache in his gut was gone. His mouth and throat felt moist and warm. He sat down in the cushion of the warm milky white mist and gazed dreamily at the scene above him.

I've got to bring Ebony here.

Next, Degu saw a small dark figure, far up on the solid white rainbow. It grew slowly as it descended, sliding down the middle until it came into clear focus. Landing at the base of the rainbow, the large being floated in front of Degu. He resembled the Cherokee ancestors with a strong, hooked nose, high cheeks and dark braided hair that fell long on each side of his bare chest. The similarities stopped there. His eyes were blinding white, with no irises or pupils. He had tattoos of various moon phases, excluding the full moon, across his forehead and around his wrinkled mouth. His shoulders and upper arms were all bone and sinew, leading down to his forearms which gradually became more laden with taupe colored scales, finally concluding with thumbs and three crooked fingers extending into long, smooth, curled black talons. Degu could see the light glint off of the razor sharp tips. The lower half of the being's body was a trail of grayish smoke. Draped over one forearm was a glossy brown oak walking cane. The warmth that Degu had been bathing in was washed away by a flood of deep cold. Degu pushed himself up and took a step back.

"I suppose that is the wisest course of action."

The voice was smooth and rich with a British curl to it. While the being spoke, gnats flew in and out of his mouth. He floated to the side and rested his torso on a large rock. Wherever he moved, the white mist parted and cleared. He propped his taloned arms atop the wooden cane. Degu stood stock still, only moving his eyes to follow this hideous creature.

"So, we meet *face* to face for the first time. How do you like me now?" the being smiled, dropped the cane and spread his arms wide like a performer preparing to take a final bow. "What's the matter? Gnats got your tongue? Well, I suppose that's better than maggots having your tongue."

With these words, the creature opened his mouth wide to display the writhing, roiling dirty yellow larvae that filled the inside. The gnats continued to swirl about. Degu released a small gasp before trapping his remaining shallow breath high in his throat.

"Well, while I would love nothing more than to linger here watching you swell further and further in me, I really don't have the time to spare. So I will get on with the business at hand. Oh! Where are my manners? I should introduce myself. I am the infamous, the notorious, the much maligned and ballyhooed Raven Mocker, at your service." With this introduction, he rolled his right arm in front of himself three times while taking the scene-ending bow. The being raised his head and eyebrows in mock surprise. "What, were you expecting someone with less refined speech; some boorish clout like I send to your world to inhabit your low rent horror films; the lumbering beasts who can only grunt and snarl. Please. Surely I deserve more credit than that." The Raven Mocker then raised his arm to his mouth and used a talon as a toothpick, scraping away a larvae that had lodged between two of his light brown teeth.

"No, I deserve much more credit than that. After all, I do create very clever advertising campaigns. And then, of course, there're your politics and religions." He flicked the loosed maggot to the ground. "Well, anyways. Here's the problem, *Degu*." Although he had no discernible eyes, Degu instinctively knew the beast was staring directly at him. "I have been *too* good, *too* accomplished in my efforts in your world. As much as I hate to admit it, your last vision, you know, the one where your El-li-si told you about her conversation with the pine and the bark beetle? As much as I hate to admit it, I am now experiencing the truth of that. *Balance* does matter. I have spent an eternity scouring your land and time, consuming all that I could, seeking to quell my insatiable appetite. I never could get quite enough though. Too many saw me for who and what I am. They resisted. They denied me my recompense. This only drove me harder."

He paused and pursed his lips. "Well, lo and behold, wouldn't you know it. We arrive at this time and it seems I have won the day. All my dogged efforts have come to this point where I have won. The balance has been tipped."

The shock that had gripped Degu was starting to be replaced by confusion. He stood up straighter but kept one foot behind and turned, ready to fight or flee as either situation presented itself.

"Because I have never before achieved this status, I suppose I never considered what consequences may arise. My, oh my, but here we are." With crossed arms, the beast shook his head and tapped a talon on his cheek. He oriented back to Degu. "What's the matter, boy? Am I not making sense to your simple mind?" The refined voice rose and blended into a shrill metallic screech before dropping back to its original quality and tone.

"Okay, here's the simpleton version: I am the Raven Mocker. I infect as many beings as I possibly can. This is my only source of sustaining myself. I am the ultimate *parasite*. My hosts do my bidding, seeking out other beings to infect with my spirit, to continue serving and feeding me. I exist in both the material and the Spirit world; always have. But lately I have become too dominant in your world. This has dramatically upset the aforementioned balance of which I spoke. A domino effect has begun that is altering the balance between the material and the Spirit world. You saw this first hand with the human-animal hybrids falling from the sky. You see it all around you with the drying of the Adanvado. I myself have never taken a distinct form as you see now evolving before you. This is not good Degu. The Adanvado is dying. Once my distinct form is completed, I will be contained. As you can clearly see, my best mercenaries have proven to be too good. The oak bark beetles are consuming everything in sight. They have gotten beyond my control. I am certain they will eventually consume me. They already mock *me* by laying their eggs in my mouth. Once I am gone, there will be no way to stop them from consuming the rest of the Spirit world. Once the Adanvado is gone, the material world will meet its quick and ugly death. Then . . . it is finished. Everything. Nothing."

The Raven Mocker laughed, paused and leaned in towards Degu. "How's that sound to you, Degu, son of Darrell and Honey Collins?"

A sharp chill pricked the back of Degu's neck. His heart was pounding; his voice a pitiful tremor. "What, what do you want with me?"

The Raven Mocker tilted backwards. "Ah, yes. What on earth would I want with a simpleton like you?"

Degu felt a narrow surge of anger rise through his sternum.

"Well, here's the thing, Degu. You were given a toy, a wooden yo-yo. You figured out that it was, shall we say, special. Without boring you with all of the details," the Mocker leaned forward again. "I need that yo-yo!"

"I don't understand. I don't have it."

The metallic screeching returned. "I know that, you pathetic rot! What did you do with it?!"

Degu's anger swelled in his chest. "How is it that you know my visions, know my parents' names? You know so much about me and yet, you don't know that my yo-yo was taken from me and is lost forever?"

The original voice resumed. "Of course I know it was taken from you the first time. It was my ravens that did this. But like I said, I've been too successful. I'm beginning to lose control over my charges. Those two ravens cannot be relied upon. And besides, I only need . . . oh never mind. Listen to me. The yo-yo is not lost forever. I will continue my search. I suspect that you may find your precious toy before I do. And if you do, you need to know that the only way to save the Adanvado and your godforsaken world is to help *me* regain the balance. I need that yo-yo to do this!"

The Raven Mocker rose and floated directly toward Degu, who jerked his arms up in front of himself. The evil presence hung in suspended motion for a moment, his acrid stench wafting over Degu. Something bulky and dark thudded at Degu's feet. "Don't look a gift horse, or Raven Mocker, in the mouth, my boy. You will need your strength to do my bidding."

The foul being cackled and then whisked to the side and away into the forest. Degu instantly felt a crushing weight on his shoulders, forcing him to the ground. The whole scene evaporated; the mist, the rainbow, the moon, even the clearing; all was gone. Degu sat forward panting. He then doubled over. The piercing hunger pains had returned. While remaining bent in two, Degu's breathing slowed and he smelled the object that the Raven Mocker had left him. It was a large, bloodied ham. Degu barely hesitated before devouring the raw meat.

Once he finished, Degu thought of Ebony. His heart sank. He smacked the sides of his head. "What is wrong with me? I should have saved half for her."

The guilt rolled through his mind like a thick bank of fog.

Chapter 12

Degu sat alone on the forest floor, his mind beginning to numb to all of the events of the past few days. Images whirred seamlessly, endlessly blurring one into the next, until he started to doze off. His head hit the ground and he startled awake.

No! I can't sleep. I can't take any more visions. I have to get up and keep moving. He pushed up to a kneeling position and rose unsteadily. He couldn't go back and face Ebony. After all that he had done, the last straw was him selfishly eating the whole ham. Surely, she would never forgive him.

The daylight was dropping before his eyes. Having no plan, Degu looked around on the forest floor for an object, any object that might help him in some manner.

While searching, Degu heard a scratching sound above in the trees. Squinting in the fading light, he saw the silhouette of the vulture guide perched on a thin branch overhead. Further up in the trees, several other large black and turkey vultures held their stately posts. Exhausted and weary, Degu was unsure if he was now in the throes of a dream. His raspy words had little push behind them. "Are you real?"

The guide spread his giant wings, lifted and floated down to the ground in front of Degu. "Your trials are far from over, Degotoga. But this is where I must leave you for now."

"No!" Delirium was settling in Degu's eyes and throat. "I can't take this madness anymore." His voice thinned. "It's too hard."

The vulture straightened and lifted his rose colored head. "Yes, it is hard. But madness and hardness are two different things, Degotoga."

The guide bobbed his head. "Of the two, which do you suppose can be remedied?"

Degu slumped and mumbled. "Neither."

"Wrong. You can accept hardness and thus reduce it. You see, hardness is a product of madness. When you accept it, you lessen its power until eventually it is gone. Even the madness transforms; though it never goes away."

The bird paused.

"I am almost out of words. I must save what remains for the last hour. Remember that you and I have spoken before."

Degu thought back upon their previous encounters. The guide continued.

"Not in this world, Degu." The vulture cocked his head slightly to one side and, in spite of the deepening darkness, a twinkle gleamed in his eye.

"Rojo?"

The vulture spoke no more, opening and thrusting his powerful wings to rise in the air. The remaining birds lifted in unison, and the entire committee filtered through the tops of the trees and away.

Degu remembered talking with Rojo in his office, when Rojo handed him the note for playing VQII. He reached into his front pants pocket. He felt the folded paper he knew had not been there since his arrival in the Adanvado. He started to pull it out but realized it was getting too dark to read. He pushed it back down and rested his hand over the top of it, feeling comforted by its presence. He breathed in deeply, feeling a mixture of promise at having found Rojo, but also lingering weariness borne of his fatigue, his encounter with the Raven Mocker, but most of all, of his ache over losing Ebony.

I'm going to have to stop and rest. I'm getting too tired to think. I'll look at the note in the morning. Besides, what are the chances I'll have another nightmare? Degu shifted and overrode the thought. *Wait a minute. I'm in the land of Madness. Of course, I'll have another nightmare. But that's all it will be.* Lying down on the firm forest floor, he recalled the words of his guide and friend Rojo. *Hardness and madness. Not the same thing. I can handle the dreams. I will be okay in the morning.* With this final thought, Degu quickly dropped into a deep sleep.

Degu opened his eyes and saw before him the bird skull man from when he first arrived in the Adanvado. "It's you," was all he could say before he suspected that he was inside of a dream. Realizing this, Degu was surprised and then unsure of what to do next.

I'm aware in my own vision.

"Yes, you are Degotoga," the skull's deep voice reverberated in Degu's head. "Your trials are making you stronger. Knowing how to walk in your visions is an important *first* step. You will need time to adjust to this new skill. There are a few things I will share to help you."

Degu stared at the creature in cautious excitement. He was thrown off by the being having lost its one remaining metal wing. Now it had two human arms filled with oozing pustules and sparse jumbles of wiry black hair.

The beast spoke again. "Allow me to properly introduce myself. I am Talanuwa, the Conjurer. Understand that I am not your friend; nor am I your enemy. I am simply here to give you the objective truth." With these words, the hulking creature's hollowed eye sockets filled with a faint light green mist.

"First, it is a privilege few humans are given; the ability to walk in their visions. Always remember that you are a guest here. Respect *everything* you see and hear in your dreams. Everything in your visions comes from Unetlanvhi, what you would call the Great Spirit, and is offered to you for your own healing."

The beast then extended its mottled right fist, palm side up.

"Second, visions frequently have more than one meaning."

The Conjurer then opened its hand. Degu stared as first rumbling bumps arose under the beast's skin, expanding and gyrating.

"Third, you do not dictate the terms of these visions. You are to receive the messages to the best of your ability. Do not try to change your dreams. Your efforts will be in vain."

Next, the skin ripped open and a torrent of the glowing red and black oak bark beetles came flooding out, dropping to the ground and fanning out to everything in the vicinity. Degu spun on his heels and began running away. He looked over his shoulder to see what was happening with the bugs. In doing so, he didn't see the small hole in front of him. He heard the snap and felt the instant surge of pain in his right ankle as he sprawled and rolled on the ground. The bark beetles were closing in on him. He panicked.

Before he could form a coherent thought, he felt himself elevating a few feet off of the ground. Suddenly, he was moving over the ground at an increasing rate of speed. The beetles were fading in the background. Degu heard the thunderous voice from Talanuwa in the distance.

"Everything is dying here in the Adanvado. The corn will be the last."

Degu continued to glide effortlessly a few feet off of the ground. He stared down in disbelief. He began to see faint colors coming into view. Within moments, he clearly saw the heads of dwarves with their arms extended above, holding him up as they ran. Their legs moved in perfect synchronicity and with little to no effort.

What are these things?

"It's *who*, not *what*," came the reply from one of the beings with his arms holding Degu just under the tip of his right shoulder. The voice was high and scratchy. Hearing this triggered Degu's memory that he was within a dream.

Degu spoke aloud. "Where are you taking me?"

There was no answer. The legs kept churning in their steady cadence.

"Look. I appreciate you guys saving me from those evil bugs, but how do I know you're any better."

Still, there was no answer.

Degu thought again about being in the dream. *This is only a dream. It's not real. I can make them stop if I want. I will just create a rolling log with my thoughts to come knock them away.*

Immediately, the running ceased and Degu slammed on the hard ground. The small beings evaporated, except for the one that had spoken to Degu. He came and stood in front of Degu's face. He had olive colored skin with wide set eyes, a broad flat nose and thick black hair parted in the middle. His braids fell almost all the way to the ground. His head was almost as large as his square-shaped body.

"You no longer deserve our help, you big ugly snit. Didn't you listen to Talanuwa? You wasted no time in trying to manipulate your vision."

Degu was trying to regain the wind that had been knocked out of him when he hit the forest floor. He also noticed his ankle starting to throb. "I, I'm sorry. I didn't think—"

"No, you did not think!"

The being leaned in closer and studied Degu's remorseful and confused eyes. His countenance softened. "I will tell you one story before I leave you," the dwarf continued. "There is a battle between two wolves, or in your case, two raptors, inside each of us. One is evil, the other, good."

Degu's breathing leveled. He rubbed the side of his swelling ankle. "Which wolf, um, bird wins the battle?" he asked.

"Neither. Or both, I suppose." The little man shrugged. "How am I supposed to know? This is your dream, Degotoga." He then smiled and vanished.

Degu lay for only a moment when he heard the rumble, felt the ground's vibration, and turned to see the dust cloud floating behind the charging horde of glowing red and black bugs. Degu held his breath steady and concentrated. He tried to get up and run but fell again when he put his weight on his injured ankle. Panic rising, he tried in vain to crawl along as quickly as he could. When the horde was nearly upon him, Degu abruptly stopped and gathered his wits. *I can do this!* he thought. *Wake up Degu. C'mon! Open your eyes!*

Chapter 13

Light flooded in. Everything was still. Degu saw he was alone in the familiar aspen forest. It was morning and he was lying in a small clearing. The sky was a deep blue and the early sun found an opening through the trees. It beamed at an angle down to him.

Degu continued to lie for a few minutes reviewing the dream from which he had just awoken. He strained to remember what the Conjurer had told him about visions. *Respect everything I hear and see in my visions.* "I guess I didn't exactly do that," he said out loud. *Everything is offered for my own good. How can this be? I saw my El-li-si get crushed by a falling tree. I've seen so much death and destruction; those possessed creatures, swarming everywhere over everything.* Degu shuddered. He then remembered the next message. *Dreams often have more than one meaning. I guess I hope that's true. But how am I to know what to believe? What to follow?* His thoughts shifted to the event-filled day before. The emotions swirled and mixed in an awkward dance in his mind. He remembered the argument and his decision to leave Ebony. His heart ached. He recalled seeing Rojo transformed as his vulture guide and felt reassured. He thought of Rojo's comment about saving his words for the final hour. *What does that mean? That sounds so dark.*

Degu sat up and wrapped his arms around his folded knees. He began to subtly rock in an unconscious effort to soothe himself. He stared into the forest. Something darted across his field of vision, moving from the back side of one tree to another. Degu lifted his head and tried to followed the blurred image moving at an improbable rate of speed; starting and stopping behind trees no more than ten feet apart. The image was angling closer to Degu. He rolled over onto his knees to rise to a standing position when the thing zipped directly in front of him.

"You?!" Degu said, recognizing the dwarf from his dream. The man was wearing a wrinkled and loose fitting off-white robe with a brown rope cinched at the waist.

"Yes. It is *me*," the forest dwarf answered; this time his voice contained a slight echo.

"But how did, you were, you were in my vision, uh, how are you here now?" Degu craned his neck and searched the surrounding sights. "Am I back in the vision? Did I never wake up?!" Degu felt the old tide of fear rising in his chest.

"Calm down Degotoga," the man said with a dismissive wave. You're not in the vision anymore. I promise."

Degu sat back, placed his hands behind him and began to push backwards.

"Don't believe me? Here, I'll prove it to you." The dwarf stepped over to the side of Degu's left leg, pulled his bare, gnarled foot back, and kicked Degu swiftly on the ankle.

"Owww!! That hurt!" Degu barked, reaching over to rub the stinging skin and bone. "Why'd you do that?!"

"Well, in your vision, it was your right ankle that snapped. I just kicked your left ankle."

"What's your point?" Degu's fear was giving way to anger.

"Try standing, big shot. If you are still in the vision, your right leg won't hold you up while you recover from my love tap."

Degu stared at the dwarf and then hesitantly rolled over onto his knees and hands and pushed up to stand. He was surprised to notice how solid his right ankle felt. Even the sting from the left ankle was subsiding.

"Enough proof for you, big guy?"

Degu looked down from his six foot seven frame to the man standing below him. This dwarf couldn't have been more than two feet tall. Degu's foot was nearly as big as this man. He had the briefest image of rearing his leg back and punting this annoying rapscallion through the trees into oblivion.

"Not your best idea, captain."

Degu snapped to attention. "What's not my best idea? And why do you keep calling me those names?"

The dwarf rolled his eyes and dropped his shoulders. "The whole booting me through the forest thing. I wouldn't advise that."

"How do you know my thoughts?"

"Who said that I could? Let's just cut to the quick here. My name is Rock. My clan and I live here in the forest. *I* know that you were brought here by El-li-si and Rojo."

"You know them? Have you seen my grandmother? Is she okay?"

"Listen to me, Degotoga. You have to get through the rest of these woods, and that's not happening without my help. Your job is to find your Wohali and bring him home. You worry about that and that only. Your El-li-si is quite capable of taking care of herself."

"But, in my vision, I saw her die." Degu pushed the last word out with almost no air behind it. This was the first time he had uttered it.

"Remember Degotoga, dreams *often* have more than one meaning and *always* come in the spirit of healing."

Degu stood with a frumpled face for a moment. He then sighed and shook his head. "Okay. What do we do now?"

Rock spread his stumpy fingers wide and the map scroll appeared.

120

"Hey! You found my map!"

"Yes, well, you really shouldn't leave things lying about; especially things essential for your survival and successful mission."

Rock cut his eyes up at Degu as he straightened out the parchment. When Degu looked at the map, it had once again changed. It now showed the land of Madness on a much larger scale, with smaller definition of the trail and land on either side. In fact, Degu could only see the word *Roots* in tiny letters at the top edge of the map; previously, it was along the left side. *Soaring* was no longer on the map.

"We are here," Rock said jamming the fat of his thumb down in the middle of a copse of thick trees. He then skimmed his thumb over to the west boundary. "This is where we need to go. This is where you will find Wohali waiting."

"But I thought that we . . ." Degu's heart sank as he thought of Ebony. "I mean I thought that I needed to go to the place of roots and soaring. Those were the words I had written on the stand back home on the oak tree."

"The what?" Rock scrunched his wide set face. "What are you talking about?"

Degu scrunched his face back at the little man.

"Listen. You just follow me. I'll try to not go so fast. The forest has been decaying at an alarming rate, spreading from the north and east. We really don't have time to waste."

Rock rolled up the map and looked down at his feet as he started to move, seemingly willing them to go slow enough for Degu to keep pace. Degu thought of Rock's comments about the vision and about finding Wohali. Then he remembered the meeting with the Raven Mocker.

The only way to save the Adanvado and your godforsaken world is to help me regain the balance. I need that yo-yo to do this!

His last thought returned to Ebony.

"Let's go, Chief! We haven't got all day."

Degu jogged a few steps and then stopped. Rock turned and halted, clenching his jaw and flaring his nostrils.

"What's the problem, Degotoga?!"

"I need to tell . . . um, how did you . . . you seem to know my visions. Did, do you know my thoughts? I mean, did you just get the one about the Raven Mocker?" He decided not to ask if Rock knew his thought about Ebony.

Rock hung his head and shuffled back to Degu. Standing in front of him, Rock didn't bother to lean back to look up at Degu. He talked in a monotone echo directly to Degu's shins.

"No Degotoga. I cannot read your thoughts. I'm only able to know your visions while you are in my forest. The whole kicking me through the woods was an easy guess. But, as far as the Raven Mocker goes, I don't need to know your thought. My family and I watched the whole meeting you had with him. We heard everything. We have argued non-stop about that since it happened yesterday."

Degu scrambled to sit down in front of Rock. "So what do we do? Is what he said true? I mean, what's the use of going for Wohali if everything will be destroyed?"

"Stop, stop, stop it! Listen to me! We can't trust the Raven Mocker and his, his, his legion. For all we know, he is just setting up this whole ruse to get his hands on the yo-yo. Whatever it is about that thing, it must be critical for claiming power over both worlds."

Degu reached over and draped his massive hand on Rock's shoulder and side. "So then, we have to go find it first!"

"No. That's what *he* wants you to do."

Rock then shifted his eyes back and forth and leaned in closer to Degu and whispered. "He's probably got his minions tracking your every step. And besides, the yo-yo is safe and sound."

Degu did a poor job of copying Rock's whisper. "You know where it is?!"

"Shush," Rock grumbled. "The yo-yo is safe. We need to get you to Wohali."

Degu reflected for a moment and then stood up. Rock smiled, turned, and began moving. Degu held his place. After a short distance, Rock looked back. Once more, his face cinched into a growl as he stomped back.

"What now?!"

"I can't follow you. At least not in that direction."

"And just why is that, Mr. Big Stuff?"

"In the vision, you told me about the two wolves, or raptors."

"Uh-hum." Rock's face softened and he held his chin in his hand.

"Well, I did something wrong. And you probably know what that is."

"Go on."

"Your clan lives in these woods. You probably saw what happened with me and my friend Ebony. I guess you saw the vision where I, um, where she kissed me."

"Yes."

"And you probably saw us argue, and me . . ." Pools of tears welled in his eyes. "I was hurt, but mostly I was afraid, Rock! I shouldn't have left her! I love her! And I know she loves me. I just know it. We hadn't said it, but it's still true." The tears ran haltingly in crooked paths down the sides of his face.

Rock crossed his arms and smiled sympathetically. This time there was no echo when he spoke. "What do you want to do, Degotoga?"

"I don't understand everything here. But I do know that what I did was wrong. And I can try to fix that. Ebony and I started out together. We were supposed to help each other. I now know with everything in me that I need to find her. Finding Ebony and making things right with her is the most important thing."

Degu nodded to himself.

"I will worry about Wohali, and the Adanvado, and the yo-yo; I will worry about all of those things later."

Rock's grin grew. He paused and then chuckled and slapped Degu across his shin. "Okay, Big Guy. Now you're talking!" His face then drew inward. "You are choosing the right path my friend. It's the hard path, but the right one."

Degu scratched his bald head and offered a half smile. "Like I haven't been on the hard path already?"

All lightness had vanished from Rock's face. "Things are worsening by the hour, Degotoga. We're going back into the heart of Madness; actually back to the beginning. We're going into the face of death. It will take us all day to get there. That's where you will find your Ebony."

Degu furrowed his eyebrows. "But why? I don't understand. Is Ebony okay?"

"What's there to understand in the land of Madness?" Rock said as he waddled past Degu and into the thick of the forest.

Degu briefly panicked at the notion of going back, and finding Ebony in peril. He squeezed his eyes shut and shook his head. He called the image of Ebony's deep, onyx eyes to mind. *I'm gonna make things right, Ebony.* He rubbed his face, exhaled deeply and jogged to catch up to Rock.

The odd pairing of the lumbering giant and the speedy, mystical dwarf moved at a steady pace through the aspens. Degu was chatty at first, his emotions growing more charged at both the anticipation of finding Ebony but also the gnawing agitation of going backwards towards the haunting scenes of the days before. He brought to mind the words of his guide and friend Rojo: *Madness and hardness are not the same thing. I can do this.*

Talking seemed to help pass the time and level his anxiety. He realized he had never done this in the past. He was momentarily amused as he thought, *I bet I've talked more today than I have in the past year combined.* He flooded Rock with questions about his clan and how they could see others visions in the forest, about how they could move at such speed. Rock indulged him, patiently answering his questions. Degu finally asked him about the yo-yo.

"Can you tell me now about the yo-yo? How do you know it's safe?"

At this, Rock stopped abruptly. "I told you. *He* has eyes and ears everywhere." He then stood on his tiptoes and beckoned for Degu to bend over. He whispered into Degu's ear.

Rock peered at Degu and then cut his eyes to scan the surrounding woodlands. Degu followed suit. Looking around, he was shocked to see the remarkable changes in the forest since yesterday. The spindly chalky white aspen trees now appeared jaundiced. There were no signs of the oozing clear orange sap. The grasses covering the forest floor were brittle and ash blonde, and intermingled with shriveled dark brown leaves from the bare branches. Looking up, Degu could see much more of the sky. The deep blue had been replaced by a blazing yellow glare.

The two resumed their trek with less and less talking. Degu noticed an increase in the number of dead branches and fallen limbs along the path. Rock had little trouble navigating these despite his small stature. Degu, on the other hand, was slowing down as he frequently got snared or tripped over them. The oppressive sun was at its apex in the sky. Degu felt the dry gristle in his throat and the stab of hunger in his gut.

"No time to stop and eat or drink," Rock said. "We'll eat on the go."

"Wha, wait," Degu said, continuing to stumble along. "I thought you said you couldn't read my mi—"

"Here, have some granola. It will give you energy." Rock pulled a small purple velvet pouch from his rumpled tunic and handed it to Degu. Degu grabbed the bag and uncinched it. Like a baby bird, he tilted his head back and dumped the contents into his gaping mouth. Immediately he spit it out on the ground.

"Hey! That stuff is valuable! What are you do . . .? Ahhh. I forgot." Rock then fumbled in his tunic and pulled out another velvet pouch. This one was crimson, containing a small lump. "Sorry 'bout that. Here, this is what you need." He handed the bag to Degu, who reached out more slowly this time, staring first at Rock and then at the pouch.

Instantly he smelled the raw meat inside. "What is it?"

"It's venison. Deer meat. My clan only eats grains. Your clan, um, well you just need the protein. I'm sorry it's such a little piece. Better than nothing though."

Rock looked away.

Degu's puzzlement was overruled by his hunger. He jerked open the bag and once more deposited the small chunk of flesh into his gaping maw. He was surprised at how much effort it took to chew the rubbery meat. It was making his jaw sore. After swallowing the first bite, he realized how dry his mouth was.

"Can I have something to drink?" he garbled.

Rock shook his head, not bothering to look at Degu. "I'm sorry. Everything, I mean everything is drying out. Our last stream dried up this morning. We'll have to go without."

Degu's mouth fell slightly open as he consider Rock's words. *Everything really is dying.* He again scanned the land in front of them. There were fewer and fewer standing trees. It was beginning to look like a tornado had leveled the forest. He noticed various odd shaped lumps further in the distance. He smacked his dry, cracked lips before returning to chewing the last bite of the meat. *At least I have this. I must keep my strength. I have to find Ebony!*

The pair worked their way through the increasing debris. Degu noticed that Rock was beginning to labor in his pace. Soon, the fallen trees were thinning and they were approaching the previously unrecognizable lumps on the ground. Degu froze in his steps.

"The animals."

He pointed and stared at all of the animals he had seen in his forest vision. Scattered about were the dead carcasses of the great and noble beasts; the mountain lion next to the sheep; the elk lying near the timber wolf; and all the rest. The scene was one of total desolation. Degu gasped.

"Rock. I saw . . . these were in—"

"In your vision. Yes, I know, Degotoga," Rock answered in a timorous voice.

This time he turned and looked up at Degu. Degu lurched back in shock. Rock's face had become ashen and shriveled; his black hair now gray and brittle. His eyes were dull. Rock looked to the sky. "The sun is descending in the east. Our time is drawing short." He was wheezing now. "C'mon. We've got to keep moving."

Degu hesitated. He was losing his resolve. His hands trembled. His head pounded. His vision blurred; all the effects of his dehydration. He felt a muted thwack across his lower right calf. He looked down to see Rock listlessly looking up at him.

"I said, c'mon man. We've got to get there before sunset."

Degu lifted his eyes and looked beyond the fallen trees and dead animals. Everything appeared to abruptly stop in the far distance. He started to point and ask if that was the destination, but then dropped his arm and slogged forward. Degu and the forest dwarf continued now in weakened silence.

Chapter 14

The sun had nearly set when Degu stepped over the last remaining fallen tree and surveyed the barren field in front of them. He turned his head to the side and down to ask Rock a question. He was surprised to see that the dwarf had remained behind the prostrate tree. "Is this it? Uh, why are you standing behind the tree?"

Rock struggled to pull himself up onto the trunk to face Degu. "Listen to me, Degotoga. This is the end of the forest. I cannot go outside of its boundaries. You have to go the rest of the way on your own. And you have to go tonight. There's no more time. When the sun rises tomorrow, it will be the last day."

Degu interrupted. "But where am I going? What am I supposed to look for? How will I find my way in the dark? Where's Ebony? What about the yo-yo, and Wohali, and El-li-si, and, and, and—"

"Calm down and listen to me, Degotoga! You need to follow the—"

KABOOM

A crack of thunder sounded and the sky streaked with splintering lightening. The sharp fracturing lines zipped down to the ground a few feet away from Degu. A cloud of dust and dirt swirled then wafted back down, revealing the Raven Mocker. He hadn't changed from his previous appearance with Degu, with the exception of now having fully formed legs and feet. He was wearing a long-tailed formal black blazer with no shirt, his gnarled talons protruding out of the ends of the sleeves; a red cummerbund covered his waist, overlaying the top of his black dress pants. Whatever his feet may have been were stuffed into black leather shoes that curled into three tips each. An unusually long black top hat sat high on the crown of his head. The deep crevices around his mouth smoothed as his smile grew wider. The blinding whites that were his eyes bore into Degu.

"Good evening, Degu." His voice was warm and liquid.

"Degotoga! Don't listen to him!" Rock's words were dry and gravelly.

"Shut up, you fool!"

The Raven Mocker opened his mouth wide and out poured his legion of glowing black and red oak bark beetles. They streamed down his neck, torso and legs and across the ground to Rock. The bugs flooded over Rock's body and head, consuming him in seconds. Just before they completed their task, he called out, "Degotoga! Remember Rojo's gift!"

With these words, Rock vanished. The swarm of bugs shivered in a frenzied delight on the tree trunk where Rock last sat. They then spread out and consumed the rest of the fallen tree.

The Raven Mocker looked on, his arms crossed in cool detachment. "Now, where were we? Ah, yes. I was just wishing you a good evening before I was so rudely interrupted by that foul runt."

The Raven Mocker sauntered over closer to Degu. "How do you like me now?"

Degu stared in focused disdain. "He was my friend."

"Oh, pish posh," the Raven Mocker said with a wave of his hand. "Those forest gnomes only think of themselves. He probably told you some horrible story about me just to cover the fact that he stole the yo-yo. He was trying to lead you away, send you on some wild chase for your precious Ebony, so that he could then keep the yo-yo for himself. Listen, Degu. I've already bared my soul, as it were, to you. I've conceded that I am your nemesis, at least historically so. But we are in unprecedented times. Everything will cease to exist, including you and me and your precious Ebony, if you don't help me restore the balance. For once and once only, you and I are allies,

Degu."

Degu's eyes remained fixed on the vile form before him. He stole a glance at the bugs still swarming on the ground and then set his stare back on the Raven Mocker. He pulled in his bottom lip and remembered the Raven Mocker's words about the bugs consuming their Master once he was fully formed.

The fiend followed Degu's eyes and straightened his posture. "Yes, I think it's only a matter of time before these insidious creatures turn on me. Therefore, you and I had better get going."

"Where are we going?" Degu was now grinding his teeth.

"Why, we're continuing your journey to find your precious Ebony."

"I thought you said the yo-yo was with Rock."

"I didn't say he had it on him," the Raven Mocker chuckled. "Clearly he did not or we would have seen it fall out when my beetles had their meal."

Degu's face turned red as he clenched his fists.

"No, I suspect that he and his shunted little clan snuck it out of the forest. Who knows, maybe they convinced your vulture friend, or maybe one of those good-for-nothing ravens to carry it away for a time. No, I have a suspicion we will find the yo-yo when we find your precious Ebony and the others."

Dusk was settling more deeply into shadows with the suns final descent. Degu could now see little around him.

"I suggest you stay close to me, Degu. The moon has rotated back to the night sky and was full last night. Tonight begins the new moon. There will be no light to travel by. My iridescent companions will lead the way."

Degu turned to see a pulsing tide of glowing red bugs, like flowing lava, streaming alongside him and the Raven Mocker.

The beastly glow emanated just enough for Degu to see the outline of the Raven Mocker walking in front of him. He was sufficiently confused by the Raven Mocker's words. Degu instinctively knew not to trust him but did believe he would help deliver him to Ebony and thus decided to follow him. His throat felt as dry as his cracked lips. His headache worsened. He struggled with the thought of asking the Raven Mocker for food and water.

"Um." He wasn't sure of what to call the monster. "Can I have some water, and, and something to eat?"

The Raven Mocker only rotated slightly while continuing to walk. "You will address me properly when you speak to me."

Degu felt the blush rise in his cheeks. "Um, sir, may I have some water and food. I don't think I can go much farther if I don't—"

The Raven Mocker pivoted abruptly on his heels. Degu could see the reflection of the bugs red glow dancing in his eyes.

"Sir is what you call a male who is your elder. While it is true that I am much, much older than you, I am no common man!"

The Raven Mocker then dropped his shoulders and exhaled loudly. "You will address me as Master."

Degu's heart pounded in an alternating rhythm with his head. He again clenched his jaws and fists. *Keep it together Degu,* he told himself. *You've got to get to Ebony.* He drew in a deep breath. "Master, may I have some food and water?"

The Raven Mocker stood, his amused smile barely visible in the low red light. "There. That wasn't so hard, was it, Degu? One simple word, and now you shall be replenished."

The Raven Mocker reached one claw into an inner pocket in his coat and produced a leather pouch. He tossed it at Degu, who clumsily caught it in the dim red glow. "There is enough raw meat in there to tide you over. You will also find a small fruit. Anytime you squeeze it, water will dribble out from the hole in the top. DO NOT lose this fruit. You will get no more if you do."

Degu snarled, his contempt pushing higher in his throat. He opened the pouch and pulled out the smooth round fruit. It was all but invisible in the dark shadows. Degu cocked his head back, lifted the fruit to his mouth and squeezed. At first the water came out almost as a mist spray, teasing his barren tongue. He pressed with greater force and the water flowed. Some dribbled down and around his hand and forearm, some streamed directly into his mouth and throat. The feel was disorienting. Degu had dulled to the severity of his dehydration. His body now jerked alert. His mind quickened, his eyes became sharper so that he could almost see clearly in the dark. He continued to drink it in. He didn't bother to question how this fruit could magically produce water unendingly. After drinking his fill, Degu put the fruit back in the bag and grabbed a handful of the raw meat. He scarfed it down, barely slowing to chew. At first he felt the rise of energy in his body replacing the pervasive ache, then he felt the nausea surge in his stomach and chest. He doubled over and threw up much of the undigested meat. His stomach racked in pain.

Did this monster poison me?!

"No, Degu. I did not poison you," the Raven Mocker said, smacking his lips. "How stupid of you to wolf down your food and water like a mongrel dog after having so little to eat and drink on your journey. Next time, maybe you will remember this." He then turned and began walking.

Degu stood and wiped the bile and mucous from his mouth. As violent as his throwing up was, he quickly recovered. He refocused, pictured Ebony in his mind and started following the Raven Mocker again.

"Seeing as we have all night to travel before we reach our destination, maybe we should make the best of it. Hmm? What do you say, young man? Surely we can have some convivial conversation to pass the time." The Raven Mocker barely paused before continuing. "Of course, I already know all about you. Maybe I'll share a bit more about me. I do have a number of redeeming qualities."

Degu stared into the broad shoulders of the beast in front of him. As the Raven Mocker continued to prattle on, Degu noticed a faint light beaming down and reflecting off of the shiny velour of the demon's jacket. He turned and looked up while continuing to walk. The new moon was imperceptible, but Degu could see where it was. And he could see the thinnest arc sprouting from it.

The white rainbow!

He followed the arc from the moon to the demon's back and then watched as it bounced off the jacket and pointed directly at Degu's right front pants pocket.

Rojo's letter!

He recalled Rock's final words, deftly reached his hand into the pocket and felt the creased paper. He slid it out and noiselessly unfolded it. Degu's sharpened vision plus the faint ray of light from the rainbow were enough. He read the words:

This vision quest is yours alone.

Silence will now serve you. Your words will only betray you.

You have all you need for flight.

Feed yourself in the heart of That which you disdain.

It holds the key to your quest.

Degu's mouth fell open. *What the hell is this?! I am out here following the devil himself. I've lost my grandmother, Ebony, Rock, and you want to give me some kinda code I have to figure out?! How dare you, Rojo!* Without thinking he crumpled the paper and threw it on the ground behind him. The noise was enough to draw the Raven Mocker's attention. He stopped and turned around.

"What was that?"

"Huh? Oh, that was me reaching for the pouch to get more to drink," Degu replied.

The Raven Mocker hesitated and scanned the area faintly lit by the red glow. "Don't you forget, boy. We work together on this. If I don't get the yo-yo, we all die," he said with a cool edge. Silence hung in the air.

"I got it . . . Master."

Degu stepped forward and brushed past the demon and trudged ahead following the pulsing red line snaking into the distance.

The Raven Mocker quickly caught up and kept pace beside Degu. "So, where was I? Now that I've shared with you some of my better qualities, why don't we get down to the business at hand? We need to find the yo-yo. I'm certain that since Rock was bringing you in this direction that the yo-yo will be waiting for us at our final destination. But where? And with whom? Maybe you can help me figure this out, Degu."

Degu was still fuming from the note he read and was not listening to the Raven Mocker.

"Degu? Degu, are you listening to me, boy? Tell me what Rock was whispering in your ear while you were in the forest!"

Degu clenched his jaw. "He said that my Wohali was—"

A rush of sound filled Degu's head. Through his anger and anguish, he heard a cacophony of voices: his parents, El-li-si, Rojo, Ebony, Talanuwa, Rock. The crescendo of noise aligned in an indecipherable high pitch. Degu clasped his oversized hands around his ears and bald head.

Suddenly there was nothing.

"Degu! What is the matter? You must understand the gravity of our situation. It's not only you and me. It's everyone. Even your precious Ebony. Your Wohali was what? What?" The Raven Mocker's voice faded into the background as Degu saw the words of Rojo's note in his mind.

This vision quest is yours alone.

Fine, Degu thought. *I'll make it my own!*

With this, Degu sprinted off into the darkness away from the Raven Mocker and his glowing horde of minions. He was running at full speed with long pounding strides into the complete darkness. After a few minutes he glanced backwards. He saw the red curving stream following. He realized the Raven Mocker was not far behind. He pushed ahead with another burst but eventually began to tire. He heard the low decibel thrum of the possessed beetles gaining on him. He willed himself to keep going. When he finally looked back again, he stumbled and fell, tumbling over and sprawling out on his stomach. He was completely spent.

This is it, he realized. *The demon bugs will cover me in a moment. Just like with the tree, just like with Rock. It's over.*

Degu then heard a familiar thrust of wings and felt the swish of cool air press down on him. Simultaneous tugs on the backs of his lower pant legs and at the tops of his shoulders suddenly lifted him into the black night sky. He watched as the snaking red glow below stopped and became more and more distant. Degu knew it was Rojo and his companions who were carrying him. He was washed in relief, then confusion, then anger.

"I thought you said I had to do this on my own?"

There was no answer.

"Oh, *that's* right. I'm supposed to be *silent*. My words will only betray me now."

Wait, Degu realized, *my words almost did betray me.*

He took a few deep breaths to clear his mind. He was still confused by the note, but began to release the anger that had been binding him. Gazing ahead he could see the first glimmers of the rising sun on the new day. *The last day,* he recalled Rock saying. Despite the implied significance, Degu was so exhausted that he fell fast asleep in the cradling talons of his mid-air escort.

Chapter 15

Moments later Degu opened his eyes. The room was out of focus for a few seconds. He recognized the feel of his high school history textbook matted against his face. He sat up and shook his head. *Wow! That was one seriously insane dream.* He scanned the room to reorient himself to reality. His dad's workshop appeared to be in order. He glanced over his shoulder to see the narrow cot, beige blanket and puffed pillow waiting for him.

It really was just a dream. I wonder what time it is. I had to be asleep for a while.

He rubbed his neck expecting to feel a kink from the awkward sleeping position and was surprised that it was okay. He reached up to scratch his head and froze. His bald head was rough and wrinkled. Degu jumped up and jerked around. *Where's a mirror?*

Panicked, he bolted out of the workshop door. Immediately he was blinded by the sun and the cold morning air. He held his arm, folded at the elbow, over the front of his eyes. In this shading, Degu's eyes darted to and fro. He saw nothing but woods. His home was gone. There was no main road at the end of his driveway. For that matter, there was no driveway; just a deeply rutted dirt path meandering in front of him. He spun around to look at the workshop again. It was a small log cabin with ashen timbers and a rusted red tin roof.

Degu closed his eyes and tried to focus. *This is another vision. I'm in a dream.*

He tried to remember what his life was like in reality but couldn't. He only knew he was inside of his own mind. Slowly a few thoughts formed. Distant memories of a few learnings came to him: *Respect everything you see and hear in your dreams. Visions frequently have more than one meaning. You cannot change your dreams.*

Degu opened his eyes to see a procession of rickety horse drawn wagons plodding along the path in front of him. There were clusters of Native Americans moving mechanically beside the wagons. No one spoke.

Where am I? Degu thought as he began to walk and then jog alongside the wagon train. No one seemed to notice him. Up ahead he heard wailing. He ran forward and came upon a young girl, probably no older than him. She was kneeling and crying over a lifeless form on the ground. Over her, a soldier was looking down upon the pair from his healthy brown paint horse. He sat erect and faceless in his stiff black jacket outlined in bright gold embroidery. Degu slowed and then dropped down beside the girl. Her face was covered by her dirty hands and tangled black hair. He saw that she was pregnant.

Degu looked down at the dead body. It was an older lady. Her face was marked with deep crevices that Degu somehow knew were not there even a few months before. Her lips were a pallid blue with a small trickle of drying blood seeping from the corner of her mouth. Her white floral print dress was tattered and stained. He realized that she was probably much younger than she appeared.

"Wha, what happened?" he asked the young girl.

She paused from her sobs and looked up at Degu. He was shocked. When she had pulled back her matted black hair, he was staring at Ebony. All of his memories of the Adanvado came flooding back in at once.

"Ebony! I can't believe it's you!"

For a moment, Degu forgot that he was in a vision. "Ebony, I can't believe I found you. I'm, I'm, Ebony, I'm so sorry that I ran away. I was just, I was afraid and I—"

"My name is not Ebony," the girl spoke in halting English. "I am Amadahy. This is my mother, Ama. We are Cherokee."

"Alright. Quit yer bellyachin'. We got ta git goin'. We got several more miles 'fore we git ta Ataya Lake." The soldier pulled out his coiled black leather whip and rubbed his hands over it. Degu sat dumbfounded as he watched the girl rise, turn and walk away.

"Boy, I told ya to git up! I haint a tellin' you agin!" He flicked the whip loose and was beginning to draw it back.

Degu quickly rose and held his open hands up in front of him. The soldier snarled and pulled back on the horse's reins causing it to take a few steps backwards, suggesting he was intimidated by Degu's size and strange demeanor.

Degu continued holding his hands up for a few steps while looking ahead for Amadahy who was now walking alone amidst the other clusters of Cherokee. He hurried to catch up to her. Walking next to her, he searched for what to say, what to ask. He remembered from his history book that they were walking on the Trail of Tears. Amadahy kept her gaze down and forward, with a blush rising in her cheeks. Her hands rested on her protruding belly. Degu realized that it must have been inappropriate for her to be seen talking with another man.

"Um, where's your, uh, where's your husband?"

She didn't break from her forward stare. They walked for a time in silence before she answered. "He is dead. They shot him and left him to die on the road."

Degu's mouth dropped open. Before he could form a response, he saw two more lifeless bodies lying beside the path. He was horrified. Amadahy's expression never wavered.

"This is madness!" He fumbled in his mind. "We have to at least give them the dignity of a decent burial."

"Yes. But the soldiers do not let us. My people's spirits will remain here, restless, unable to go home."

"But, but . . ." Degu's anger swirled and pitched. He started to charge at the soldier who had ridden past them. He heard the voice of the conjurer, Talanuwa.

You cannot change your dreams, Degu.

He felt straight-jacketed by his anger. Just then, Amadahy reached over and touched his forearm. "I know you are a healer sent to my people. Whatever you do, please remember my Ama and me," she looked down at her bulge, "and my children."

Degu was speechless. "I, I, I'm no—"

A gunshot rang out. Degu jerked his head over and saw that several shirtless soldiers were riding in circles keeping the reins in one hand and clumsily holding their pistols and half empty liquor bottles in the other. They had arrived at what Degu assumed was Ataya Lake. There was a flurry of activity and commotion. The Cherokee were climbing into the wagons to attend to the sick and dying while the soldiers frolicked and drank, dancing around a large bonfire. Degu followed the arc of an empty bottle that splashed into the lake. There he saw other floating debris that had been tossed in by the soldiers, empty bean cans and soiled rags.

He looked further out in the water and saw a small island in the center. Anchored there was a resplendent, giant oak tree. Immediately to the left, Degu saw a lone figure, an elderly woman sitting bareback on a strapping silver steed. *The Oak! And that's the horse from my first vision! The same one that I saw when it was much older running away with El-li-si.*

He squinted to see more clearly. *El-li-si! Is that you?*

Degu's heart quickened. He sprinted towards the edge of the lake.

"Hey!" The soldier who had yelled at Degu charged after him. Degu ran faster. The next moment, he felt the jerk of the whip as it wrapped around his neck and flipped him backwards. He lost consciousness the moment his head slammed against the hard ground.

Chapter 16

Degu awoke holding his throat. He was lying on the hard cracked ground. A slight breeze had tossed red clay dust into his mouth. He coughed and sat up rubbing his eyes. The sun was low in the early morning sky, bright orange and yellow spikes radiating out from its pinkish center. He remembered the night before and the flight with the vultures. He knew that he must have slept only for an hour or so. *What a dream. But wait a minute! I think I understand Ebony's quest now! Maybe I was given that vision so that I can help her.*

He looked around for the vultures and saw that he was alone.

Where did they go?

He then thought of the Raven Mocker and his evil beetles. He scrambled to his feet and strained to see in all directions. Accepting that he was alone and in no immediate danger, Degu relaxed and sought to gather his thoughts.

Today is supposed to be the final day. From all that I've seen and heard, the Adanvado really is dying. I have no idea where I am. As far as I can see there is nothing but flat dry land. Ebony is probably somewhere to the north trying to help the Shadows. How am I supposed to know which way is north?

He scrunched his face trying to think of a plan. *Wait a minute! I remember Rock saying the sun set in the east here!*

Degu surveyed the land again and pointed towards the shimmering orb rising from the west. *Then that must be west.* Degu rotated his arm clockwise 90 degrees. *This must be the direction I need to go.*

Despite there already being a stiff, hot breeze, Degu moved forward in purposeful strides, his sight due north and unbroken. He knew there was nothing to protect him from the rising heat. There was nothing to do but go forward at a steady pace and manage the heat, exhaustion, dehydration and hunger as best he could. The remainder of this leg of the vision quest was his alone. He would keep moving, staying alert for something, anything that would show itself. He was convinced he would find Ebony and help her and the Shadows. In all of the emotion lingering from his dream, he completely forgot about Wohali and the yo-yo.

Degu's heart surged when he remembered seeing El-li-si in his dream. *She's alive!* He gasped and clutched his shirt. *El-li-si!*

He cried tears of joy, feeling the bereft weight of her loss lift from his chest. With all of the insanity surrounding him the past few days, he hadn't taken the time to think more about her possible death. It just clung to him like a wet wool blanket. Now, she was alive. He just knew this to be the truth of his dream. This stirring propelled him, and his pace quickened.

Staring ahead into the mind numbing sameness of the barren land he was crossing, he thought back on seeing his grandmother running off in the distance when he first arrived in the Adanvado. He recalled the stallion that ran alongside her, the same one that appeared in both his first and last vision; the one that dived into the horde of beetles that were devouring the oak tree that stretched to the sky; the one that held his grandmother high under the tree on the island in Ataya Lake. He wondered about this creature. *Who could it be?*

Degu's memory was interrupted by a bluster of dry, hot wind. The red dust flecked in his eyes. He was surprised that the irritation didn't cause his eyes to tear. He rubbed again, feeling the sharp pricks of pain under his lids. He opened and blinked several times. He looked skyward, over the top of the rising sun and imagined seeing Rojo. The image calmed and comforted him. Rojo was his true friend. Together with Ebony and El-li-si, he felt a coalescing family unit; one that offered something he had not felt before, steadfast love.

Degu paused and began to draw in a deep, cleansing breath, but his lungs and throat seized at the deep intrusion of heat and dust. He gagged and coughed, bending over at the waist. He shook his head, straightened up and started walking again.

His mind shifted to the Raven Mocker. He was certain he would encounter the craven demon and his vile hordes once more. He sought to push the wrenching image aside by revisiting each of the visions he had received while in the Adanvado. He tried to concentrate, hoping to glean a possible pattern or meaning that would help him finish what lay before him.

His frustration grew in time with the climbing heat. The wind died down, only serving to raise the heat index. He started to grow dizzy and lose focus. He was aware that his face and bald head were burning in the high sun. He reached up to wipe the sweat from his brow and stopped suddenly. His hand was dry. *No! I'm no longer sweating. Isn't this a sign of heat stroke?*

Degu squinted ahead, hoping against hope that he would see something on the horizon. Nothing. He remembered the pouch with the water fruit. He reached for his pockets. Gone. Degu swallowed, his throat spasming, causing a hacking cough.

I'm not going to make it. I can't believe this is happening!

He stumbled forward and fell to the hard ground.

NOOOO.

His vision blurred.

This can't be it.

The left side of his face slapped in the dirt.

I'm sorry Ebony. I'm so sorry . . . Rojo . . . El-li-si . . .

Degu closed his eyes. Slowly, the ground started quaking, the cracked earth underneath him widening a few inches. He felt the shift and opened his eyes to see.

Is this the end? An earthquake? The earth is going to swallow me?

He closed his eyes as his body jerked in rhythm with the tremulous ground. He barely noticed the rush of wind, hotter than the air current above ground, rising out of the fissure. In the next moment, he felt weightless. He was still shaking but noticed he no longer felt the hard ground. Degu opened his eyes and saw that he was in ragged flight. He hovered momentarily about 10 feet off of the ground before being pushed higher and forward. He noticed that his flight followed the irregular pattern of the ground opening up below him. He soon rose so high that he could no longer see the cracked lines below. He also realized that at this elevation, the air was a scrambled mix of hot and cold. It was invigorating and restoring his energy and equilibrium.

It took Degu a few minutes to adjust and figure out how to hold his body posture such that the rough turbulence would even out. He figured out that he needed to hold his long arms completely wide and taut. This helped to stabilize his flight. He then was free to explore the land below. When he first looked down he was shocked at how high he was. Immediately, his smooth flight was disrupted and he began to hurtle downwards. He panicked. His tumble accelerated. Degu fought in his mind to figure this out.

You have all you need for flight.

The words from Rojo's note came back to him. Instantly, Degu calmed. He was still falling but was now tumbling less. He remembered to hold his arms wide. The descent stopped. Degu leveled and began to climb again.

Soon he was back at his highest altitude. This time Degu kept his wits about him. He found that he could actually relax with his arms stretched out. Once more, he was feeling rejuvenated. He was aware that he couldn't see anything below. The sun was directly above him. The earth below offered no contrast. He had lost his sense of north.

How am I going to know where I'm going?

He flew for a few moments trying to sort this out when he caught the scent.

That smell!

It was the sharp scent that combined with the loamy earth.

Ebony!

He couldn't see her, but it was her scent. He knew it.

Degu looked at each outstretched arm and decided to try pulling them in slightly towards his body. When he did this, he descended, but not in the chaotic manner as before. This time, his trajectory was controlled and angular. He experimented with bringing one arm in slightly more. This allowed him to change direction. He continued his descent, covering more than a miles distance, with Ebony's scent growing more robust.

At last he saw what looked like a massive field, with neatly ridged rows hosting some sort of spiked stalks. Degu decided that this must be the dying corn field that Talanuwa spoke of. His attention was diverted to the far side. He saw two figures in a frenzied tussle. Surrounding them were throngs of pulsing red human figures.

"That's Ebony!" Degu screamed into the crashing wind. "And the Raven Mocker!"

As soon as he said this, Degu saw Ebony pitch backwards and land in a heap. She stopped moving. His heart caught in his throat. Every muscle tensed.

"NOOOO"

"Degotoga!"

"NOOOO"

Tears were streaming with spit spilling from his mouth. He began to gag.

"Degotoga! Get a hold of yourself!"

Rojo had appeared from the side, his broad two toned black and gray wings holding steady in flight. "Listen to me, Degotoga! You have to level off!"

Degu didn't break from his descent trajectory or straightaway stare to acknowledge his guide.

"I didn't get to tell her . . ." He coughed and sucked in a breath.

"Degotoga! You have to finish this the right way! Open your arms! Level off!"

Degu was heaving now, choking and sobbing. Rojo was quickly joined by the other vultures. They each nosed in and grabbed Degu by the pant legs and shoulders like they had done the night before. They slowed and leveled, continuing to hold on to their charge.

"Degotoga, listen to me. These are last words allotted to me. You are not here to save Ebony. You have to find Wohali!"

"NOOOO. She can't be dead! She just can't."

"Degotoga!"

Degu narrowed his eyes and pulled his arms in tighter. His clothes ripped free of the vultures' talons. He was now bulleting forward, aiming directly for the horrendous villain.

Chapter 17

Degu's streamlined descent began to warble, quickly degrading into a full-fledged out-of-control head over feet roll. He smacked the ground hard and skittered to a stop at the feet of the Raven Mocker. His vision blurred and his head throbbed. He struggled to regain his breath. The Raven Mocker leered down at the groaning form in front of him.

"How nice of you to join us, Mr. Collins."

The Raven Mocker smiled, this time revealing blackened teeth framed in glistening gold-plated caps. Degu rolled onto his side and curled into a fetal position. Rojo and the other vultures touched down about 20 yards away and stood vigilant. This battle truly was Degu's alone. The Raven Mocker walked once around Degu in a tight circle. He crossed his arms and shook his head.

Degu wheezed. In spite of his disorienting fall, a clear but curious thought came to him. "My name is Degotoga," he uttered. "Mr. Collins is my dad or grandfather."

"Ah yes," the Raven Mocker held up a pointed talon. "Your father, Darrell Collins. Quite the cow . . . oh, never mind. Hmm. And then there's your *grandfather;* one of my few, true nemeses."

The Raven Mocker crossed his arms at his chest once again, chuckled and shook his head. "You were a bad boy last night. And I thought we were actually getting on quite famously. I even opened up to you, shared my inner most secrets. And this is how you repay me? By running away, and then having the *audacity* to come charging at me. Tsk. Tsk."

He raised an arm and tapped himself on the cheek. "Well, I suppose I *can* see your point of view. After all, I did just impale your precious Ebony on the razor sharp stub of a dead corn stalk." He mocked Degu with an exaggerated fake frown. "Oh don't worry, my boy. She's not dead, yet. And as for your grandfather, your Eduda, the great and *fearless* Running Horse, well, I suppose he's not so high and mighty now that I have *this*."

The Raven Mocker opened the other taloned hand to reveal the yo-yo. He then squatted in front of Degu, who was still trying to clear his head from the fall. "So, it seems you have two choices, my boy. You can either try to fight me for your treasured yo-yo, or you can go and save your *precious Ebony*."

He slapped his knees and stood up, unleashing a deep guttural laugh. "Oh, this is so unfair of me," he said between lingering chuckles. "I already know you are going to choose Ebony. And even if you did choose to come after me, I have my minions. And those smart little buggers figured out how to capture and use the Shadow people. How amazing is that? Instead of coming after me, oh, okay, I did *lie* to you about that little concern of them eventually eating me. *So sorry.* Instead of coming after me, they now command the Shadows, clinging to their shadow forms. It's like I have my own little people army . . . sort of . . . not that I need it, mind you. I have the yo-yo. The sun will set soon enough and everything will cease, except for *Me!* All because of *Me!*"

The Raven Mocker clasped his talons together and offered a mocking bow to Degu. "I bid you a fond, and final, adieu, *Degu* Collins." He turned and walked away, tossing the yo-yo up in the air several times before dropping it into the inner pocket of his suit jacket.

Degu pushed himself up to a sitting position. He stared at the Raven Mocker with a feeling so raw and new that it pressed in on his chest like his dad's old two-ton truck, precariously balanced there. Despite this, his thoughts cleared, his senses sharpened.

"Dego*toga*," he said through his clenched jaw. "My name is Degotoga."

He turned and ran over to where Ebony was lying on her back. Approaching her, Degu saw her obsidian eyes fluttering, staring blankly toward the sky. They no longer held their black crystalline gleam.

He collapsed to his knees next to her and placed his giant hand gently on her ribs. The valley between his thumb and index finger surrounded the jagged yellow corn stalk that protruded six inches out of her chest. A small pool of dark red blood trickled warm against his fingers. Her shallow breath barely moved his hand.

He began sobbing.

"Degu, Degu, is that you?" Ebony's eyes remain fixed ahead. She licked her dry lips and willed in a deeper breath.

"Ebony! I'm so sorry, I'm so sorry," he cried in anguish. "If I hadn't run away. If I weren't such a coward, this never would have happened! It's all my fault!" He pulled his hand away and covered his face before wrapping his whole head in his forearms and bending over next to her head.

Ebony whispered, "Degotoga, listen to me."

She paused as he continued sobbing. Continuing to look skyward, a dull film covered her eyes as she moved her arm and felt around for him. She patted the ground first, and then found his side, shoulder and arm. She pulled at his shirt.

"Degotoga, listen to me."

He lifted up and stared at her, holding his breath for a moment.

"I understand now why my shadow told me that our quests were one in the same."

Her words brought to mind the first conversation they had about their quests. They seemed so different then. Ebony was here to help the Shadows. Degu was reluctantly here to find and save Wohali. He now felt angry that he had been told his purpose was to find the ugly beast he first encountered in the spring womb.

"If I only could have known! Maybe I could have had more courage. Maybe, maybe I would have never left you." His voice trailed off.

Ebony took another slow, deep breath. "Degotoga, listen. After you left, the ravens came back. They fished the yo-yo out of the toxic pool. You *are* here to find Wohali. Everything, the Balance, Life itself, they all depend on you finding and saving Wohali."

"But, I don't understand. You said your shadow told you that you were here to lead the Shadows home. And now you're . . . "

Ebony gagged, a spurt of blood coming out of the corner of her mouth. She gurgled through her strained whisper. "Degotoga . . . Wohali . . . the yo-yo."

Her head fell to the side away from Degu.

Degu stared in disbelief. At first, his voice came in a series of squeaks. He felt the eruption welling inside him, rising through his gut into his chest and throat. He sat up, leaned his head back and opened his mouth. The heat and force of the air thrusting out of him felt like a hydrogen bomb exploding. He was oblivious to the fact that his scream was soundless. Having released the full wave of raw emotion, he began hyperventilating. The staccato sobs roiled his lungs as he lay over the top of his lifeless love.

His breathing deepened. Degu started pounding his sledgehammer-sized fists on the ground around her body. He sat up, the crevices in his bright red face wracked in pain. Finally, the image of the Raven Mocker, standing over him, laughing uncontrollably, lifted him to his feet. His mind sharpened once more, and he looked for the fiend off in the distance. He spied him, over the heads of the beetle-infested Shadows, several hundred yards away moving at a leisurely pace. Degu rose and with clenched fists began sprinting after him.

The beetle forms closed ranks in front of Degu. He charged directly into them. The glowing masses jumped him, seeking to bring him down. Degu swung and kicked madly. In the frenzy, he could see red bugs spraying into the air. Some of Degu's punches were dislodging them from their Shadow hosts. In the midst of the fight, Degu realized that for the first time, he could actually see the Shadows. The ones that were freed from the bugs ran off to the side.

Degu recognized that there were hundreds of beetle-commandeered bodies converging on him, but he didn't care. He continued to fight with unmatched fervor. He felt a thick forearm catch him from behind, wrapping around his neck, choking him. He instinctively grabbed it with both of his giant hands and tried to pull free. Other fists continued to pummel him all about his body. With his air being cut off, Degu began to weaken. His vision fuzzed.

His hands started to slough off of the choker's arm when a flurry of black wings thrust all around him. In the next moment, Rojo and his companions were a swirling force of mayhem, exploding beetles left and right, off of their unwitting hosts. Now freed from the chokehold, Degu regained his strength and rejoined the fight. Soon, the numbers of beetle fighters dwindled. The remaining ones peeled off of their Shadows and reformed with the retreating river of glowing red and black bugs flowing away and towards their master in the fading distance.

The sun was now sitting low in the eastern sky, the direction that the Raven Mocker was heading. Degu worked to steady his heaving lungs. Rojo stepped in front of him. "These truly are my final words to you ever, Degotoga. Remember and honor *Ebony's* last words to you, and remember the note."

Degu blinked repeatedly and tried to focus. *I don't understand. I don't care about Wohali or that stupid yo-yo!*

He opened his mouth to speak but Rojo opened his broad wings and launched into flight.

Degu squatted and crossed his arms over his knees. He grunted and shook his head violently. His mind cleared. *I will honor you Ebony. I will do what you asked of me. I will find Wohali. But first, I* will *destroy the Raven Mocker.*

He rose, and strode forward, slow and deliberate at first, then quicker and lighter. The faster he ran, the lighter he felt. He soon realized that he was no longer touching the ground. He was back in flight. He stopped churning his legs and remembered to hold his arms out wide to control his speed and direction.

Flying off toward the Raven Mocker, looking down over the streaming horde of glowing red beetles, Degu was unaware of what was happening back at corn field. The newly freed community of Shadows had gathered around Ebony's still body. At the head of her body, the vultures stood. The community cleared the way and one lone Shadow walked forward in a sacred ritual, along the parted path. This Shadow reached Ebony and did a stuttering, high step dance in front of her, waving its arms. It bowed deeply, laid on top of the body and then absorbed into her.

Chapter 18

Degu spirited ahead with purpose and growing resolve. A mustard yellow fog was sitting below the setting sun. The air became more and more acrid. The wind whipped and howled. Degu was unfazed by all of this, his eyes boring into his enemy. His flight never wavered.

As he drew nearer, suddenly the stream of red oak bark beetles swelled and rose up like a giant crashing wave, creating a protective barrier for their master. Degu pulled his arms in tight by his sides, sharply increasing his speed. The terrific impact exploded bugs everywhere in a massive spray. Degu burst through the wall head first and was knocked senseless for a few moments. In his fall, he slammed into the Raven Mocker. The two tumbled over each other and ended with the Raven Mocker sitting astride Degu's chest.

"Would you challenge *Me*, you pathetic ingrate?!" The Raven Mocker closed one of his taloned hands around Degu's neck. "I am the source of all movement and change. I propel the heavens and earth. I AM ALMIGHTY," he bellowed, raising his other arm and splaying his talons.

Saying this, the Raven Mocker doubled in size. Keeping his other hand wrapped around Degu's throat, he stood and lifted Degu several feet off of the ground. He sneered at the limp boy, whose face was turning blue. "It would be so easy to kill you right this moment, but where's the fun in that? You have betrayed me, Degu. You have decided that you will no longer serve me. I cannot tolerate this state of affairs. Before this sun sets, you will swear your allegiance to me."

The Raven Mocker hoisted Degu's flopping body and walked through the low hanging smog. The stench burned in his nose. The air was so thick that he couldn't see even the arm and talons that were carrying him.

A low pitched buzzing began to swell. Degu was jerked down, banging on the hard ground. The release of the claw around his neck allowed a surge of air into his lungs. His arms were wrenched behind him and bound with a coarse rope. With his back against a post, he first felt the vibrations, then the tickling hot swarm beginning at his feet and slowly climbing up his body. Thousands of stings and bites followed the climb.

The Raven Mockers voice cut through the dense smog. "How do you like me now, Degu?!"

Degu fought in his mind to focus. *Remember the note, Degu.* *Silence will now serve you. You have what you need.*

"Huh?! I said, How do you like me now, Degu?! Answer me!" the Raven Mocker's voice reverberated.

Silence will now serve you.

The glowing red and black bugs were now up to Degu's chin. A few had crawled up the base of his neck and onto the top of his bald head. Degu stared straight ahead, focusing on his breathing, seeking to keep it steady.

Suddenly, the smog swirled away. The Raven Mocker stood several yards in front of Degu.

You impress me and disappoint me all at the same time, Degu. I take away your precious Ebony, and you continue to defy me. I cover you in my foulest stench and bury you in my beloved beetles, and yet, you still continue to resist pledging your allegiance to me. Hmmm. Well, I suppose you leave me no other choice."

The Raven Mocker stepped to the side and stretched his arm out like a game show host presenting the winning prize. Degu blanched to see Ataya Lake. This time there were no soldiers or Cherokee. The lake itself was dried up, showing heaping piles of trash strewn about. When he looked out at the island in the center of the lake, he saw the giant oak lying on its side, sheared at its base. It was withered and leafless.

The Raven Mocker smiled. "Look more closely, my boy."

Degu scanned the length of the fallen oak. Half way along, he spied the two figures from the vision, the silver steed and the elderly woman lying pinned and broken under the tree. Although Degu remained steadfast in his outward pose, he felt his heart tear.

El-li-si . . . Eduda.

A tear climbed out of the corner of one eye.

As the Raven Mocker sauntered over and held his face inches from Degu's, all that remained visible of Degu were his deep and still brown eyes. The Raven Mocker's hair was now matted and dirty, his formal wear jacket smudged and scuffed. The final sliver of the setting sun peered over the demon's shoulder. "Everyone's gone now, Degu," he said in a cloying voice. "Everyone you loooovvvvee. Evwee, wittle one. You're alllll alone now. Nobody's left."

The Raven Mocker coughed out a screeching laugh and then abruptly stopped and raised his eyebrows. "It's time to come back home, Degu. You've fought the good fight. Now is the time to serve me once again."

"My name is *Degotoga!*" he said, the bile taste in his mouth spraying onto the beast.

"My, my, aren't we the impertinent one to the very end."

The Raven Mocker leaned in even closer, reaching around to cut the rope binding his hands with one scratch from his razor sharp talons.

While doing this, in the setting shadows, Degu noticed a faint green phosphorescent glow, pulsing just underneath the Raven Mocker's thin skin. It was his heart, Degu realized.

In that moment, he remembered the final words from Rojo's note:

Feed yourself in the heart of That which you disdain. It holds the key to your quest.

Feeling the release from the rope, Degu swung his enormous arms around the Raven Mocker and tackled him backwards onto the ground. The impact knocked many of the bugs off of Degu. Before the Raven Mocker could react, Degu reared his head back, bared his teeth, and sank his whole face into the fiend's chest. Degu tore into his flesh with a speed and precision that was unnatural to his former self. With the cold, thick slime covering his head, Degu clamped onto the throbbing green heart. He felt his jaws tensing and releasing in rapid succession. He tasted both blood and meat, an unknown mixing of sweet and sour tastes. Degu was surprised that it was actually pleasant after a few bites. He continued to feast feverishly until the last of the heart was gone.

Degu was now soaked in the beast's blood and mucous. He sat back on his knees and wiped his face with his giant hand. The sun had fully set. Suddenly a bright white light spread across the land. The full moon had returned, powerfully illuminating everything around Degu. He blinked and then looked down upon the still form in front of him. His mouth gaped and a surge of electricity washed over him when he saw the big, bowed eyes under the protruding forehead, the open crevice from just off-center of the top lip up through the malformed nose, the dripping flesh from the sides of the cleft lip.

Wohali?!

Degu's body shook, a spasm of hot and cold all at once. In the midst of his bewilderment, something else caught his eye. The Raven

Mocker's gnarled hands and long, black talons receded and were replaced with hands, having two small, fragile fingers and one stub each. Lying broken on the ground next to one hand was his childhood yo-yo. One half revealed a small golden acorn, glistening against the marred, cruddy wood that housed it. Degu was mesmerized by this enchanted seed. He looked back at Wohali.

Wohali . . . Wohali . . . Wohali.

The third time the name sounded in his mind with a leveling calm. Degu didn't understand it, but he knew that he was going to be okay; more than okay. He stood, leaned over the body, and pulled it up into a deep, consuming embrace. He took in a deep breath and squeezed tighter and tighter until the body was no more, having been fully absorbed into Degu.

Degu exhaled and dusted off his hands. He glanced over towards the barren lake and the island where his grandparents lay crushed under the dead tree. He knew what he had to do. He leaned down and picked the shining acorn out of the cracked yo-yo. It was dwarfed in his massive, protective hand. He strode towards the lake bed.

Out of the dark sky and into the moon's nurturing light, five large vultures came. Degu recognized Rojo's bright red head, along with his other three companions. He was curious about the fifth one. He hadn't seen this black headed one before and yet it felt very familiar to him. This bird landed on the side of the lake and waited.

Next, Degu saw the two giant ravens, the ones that had stolen his yo-yo twice before. They came out of the dark sky and landed in the lake bed nearby Rojo and the others. They each disbursed and began milling around, eating the debris that covered the ground. Degu slowed and watched this activity in astonishment. Within a few moments, Degu could see that the animals had cleared a path for him leading directly to the center island. He glanced once more at the acorn in his hand and stepped onto the dry lake bed.

When Degu arrived at the base of the fallen oak, he peered down inside of the rotted core and expected to see the upper lengths of the trees roots. Instead he saw rich brown hummus. He felt a rush around his feet and lifted out of the tree base to see what it was. The black oak bark beetles were skittering along, no longer glowing and pulsing. They moved with the same order and deliberation as the other animals. The bugs seemed reverential, filing around him and onto the prodigious, sacred tree, consuming it as they went. Soon, all that remained was the sheared base and a line of golden sawdust, smelling sweet and musky. Degu squatted and fondled the luminous acorn for a moment, and then buried it in the center of the tree's core, pushing it deep into the soil with his thumb.

A brilliant white light overhead caught his attention. Degu shielded his eyes and looked up as the white rainbow unfurled all the way down, anchoring inside the base of the first oak. With respect, Degu took a few steps back and lowered his eyes. He heard a low pitch whinny and glanced down the length of the tree's remains. There he saw the regal steed upright with a majestic black vulture sitting solemn and proud on its back. The pair cantered over and paused in front of him. Degu dropped his head and laid his balled fist over his heart. He looked up in time to see the horse lift onto the rainbow and gallop into the sky towards the full moon. El-li-si opened her broad wings and floated off of his back and onto the lake bed to help with the cleanup. When she did, the fickle ravens cackled and flew off to the east. As Eduda receded in the distance, Degu noticed that all of the activity inside of the translucent moon had ceased. Though at a distance, he could see that all the creatures therein were bowing in Eduda's direction.

Soon, clouds crept in, surrounding but not obscuring the moon's light. Degu turned to see that the vultures had finished clearing the lake bed. They moved over to the shore. The black vulture that had been next to Rojo, lifted, swooped in low along the dry bed and began slapping her wings, creating rows upon rows of indentions in the ground. Once this was completed, she took her place next to Rojo and El-li-si.

Behind the birds, Degu saw the line of Shadows walking towards the lake bed. Each one paused and bowed, first to the new black vulture, then in Degu's direction, before going and lying down, each one in a different open depression in the lake bed. When the last one lied down, a stout wind arose. It blew the golden sawdust from the first oak on top of the Shadows, covering them in their graves.

Then it started to rain. With the moon and its rainbow still visible, Degu ran along the path with the graves on either side. He noticed the spreading bulge of roots running just beneath the surface. When he reached the lakes outer shore, the rainfall became torrential. Standing beside the new black vulture, Rojo and El-li-si, he turned to see the lake bed quickly filling. As the water level rose, he saw the first shoot of the new oak sprout up and out of the base of the first oak on the center island. It climbed along the moon's white rainbow, reaching to the sky, stretching out with budding, light green shoots of leaves dancing out of the new branches.

The rain stopped. The skies cleared. Degu saw another rainbow appear out of the back side of the moon, touching down over the distant horizon. Standing drenched on the shore, he felt a warmth at his back. He turned to see the new day's sun rising rapidly from the west. He could see two golden amber rainbows leading out of its center and tethering to the land in the distant north and south. His chest eased and expanded. He glanced down at the black vulture next to him and realized he was staring at his own reflection in the soft inky well of her eyes. Although he felt like he had dropped into a pit of downy feathers, with some settling in his mouth, this time there was no fuzziness. His heart pulsed with the conviction of a man having found his way home.

"I love you, Ebony."

The grand black vulture spread her wings and held them in a stately pose, as if she were receiving the fullness of his love and returning it in the subtle sway of her black on gray feathers.

Chapter 19

Degu's eyes slowly open. Lying on his back on the makeshift bed in his dad's workshop, he became aware of the dampness of his clothes and the sheet covering him. He looked around the shop and reoriented himself to the familiar surroundings. The air was cool and crisp. He shivered.

He saw a singular shaft of morning sun beam through the window and was immediately reminded of the sun's ropes, one of the last images from his dream. *It was so very real. Was it all just a dream?*

Although the damp and cold clung to him, he was aware of the contrast with the warmth he felt inside. He sat up, feeling a growing confidence that he had just had his first vision, or collection of visions. For the first time he felt certainty, a belief in who he was and what he was.

I am Cherokee.

He couldn't wait to go to school and tell his friend Rojo. He would have to leave a little early to allow the time needed to tell the whole dream. This was fine as Rojo always came in early on Mondays to check on the weeks various tasks. Rojo would get a kick out of being a grand and wise turkey vulture in Degu's vision. He shook some of the lingering moisture off of his hands, curious about how he had gotten so wet. He rubbed his eyes and then reached up to scratch his head. This was an ingrained habit formed from the itch that sometimes accompanied his alopecia. His hand slid across his bald, wet head.

Degu froze.

His eyes darted back and forth while he tried in vain to get traction in his thoughts. *What happened to me?!* He looked down. Rather than the familiar faded blue hoody, he saw that he was wearing a dingy white tee shirt and scuffed black jeans. His mind racing, Degu tried to find his way into reality.

What day is it?

He thought of his cell phone on the small plastic stool next to the cot. Fumbling with it at first, he finally was able to push the side button to light the display screen. He tried several times without success. *The battery must be dead.*

Degu scanned the room, searching for his phone charger. Just as he spied it, he froze again. Right next to the white plastic cord, sitting on the table by the window, lay his open American history book with a round wooden form on top. He moved slowly, eyes widened, and approached the inanimate object. His childhood toy yo-yo was on the torn textbook. The page it rested on was titled, 'Trail of Tears: Indian Removal Act of 1830'. Time suspended as he picked up the yo-yo and eyed it more closely. It was smaller than he remembered, and duller. It did seem to emit warmth the longer he held it. He pulled the loose slip-knotted string over his middle finger. With his large hand dwarfing the toy, Degu was surprised the string fit. Opening his hand, the yo-yo rolled off the end of his finger and down the line. The resulting melodic hum pulled him into a meditative trance. The toy bobbed down and curled back up and into his hand. He released it a second time and the harmonic sounds expanded. He dropped it once more. This time the hum rose to an almost ear piercing pitch.

Wooooo-haaaa-liiiii seared the air. Degu grimaced at first, then softened and smiled.

No way all of this is real.

Seeking to reorient to this world, the *new* world, he instinctively plugged in his charger and turned on his phone. He jiggled it, waiting for the display screen with the date and time to appear. Finally, the screen with a picture of a light blue sky came into focus. Instead of the familiar image of a perfectly round golden-yellow sun, he saw the screen display both a sun and full moon, each with two extended rays coming off and down to the ground. The displays usual white letters and digits popped up.

Saturday, October 18th, 7:05a.m.

Five full days had passed. Degu laid back down with a swirl of images rolling through his inner vision like an internet video menagerie. The scenes of the underwater spring; the soles of El-li-si and Rojo's feet; Talanuwa; the spirit world creatures all scrolled across his mind's eye in an ever quickening line. The ravens, his grandparents, Rojo and Ebony, the Shadows. He had a faint awareness of the Raven Mocker, but couldn't recall what he looked like. Wohali . . .

What happens now? He put the phone down and sat up.

Okay, let me think for a minute. I've been in two different worlds. It looks like I'm back in the, what did Talanuwa call this? The material world? Okay, I have to make sense out of all of this. From what I remember, everything is now balanced again in the Adanvado. The rains came, the Shadows are finally at rest. I have claimed my own Shadow, Wohali. Does this mean I died!?

Rather than alarm, Degu's thought held only curiosity. *And what about El-li-si? And Ebony? Did she exist only in my vision?* This thought pained Degu. He decided to go and look for his parents.

He grabbed his cell phone and yo-yo and ran out of the workshop. He burst into the house and whisked past his mother, who was sitting at the table smoking and reading the morning paper. For a moment, he considered that if he were dead, his mother would not be able to see him. As it was, she barely registered his presence. He sprinted down the hall, into his empty bedroom. El-li-si's belongings were conspicuously absent. He pivoted to go back towards the kitchen and his mother when he smacked into his father. This knocked his dad back several steps into the hall and caused Degu to drop the yo-yo.

Darrell was carrying El-li-si's large brown plaid cloth suitcase. "Whoa, Nelly!" his dad said in an almost falsetto voice. "Looks like somebody is feeling better. What you doin' tearing around in here?"

"Dad!"

Degu blurted out before remembering his place. The delayed impulse was to return to the nearly mute status he typically maintained with his parents.

Darrell adjusted his grip on the suitcase and regained his composure. He looked down and saw the yo-yo at his feet. He leaned over, scooped up the dull inanimate object and tossed it lightly a few times in the air. "Looks like you dropped somethin', Son."

With a gleam in his eye, he handed the yo-yo back to Degu.

"D, D, D, Dad? Are you the, are you one of the ravens?"

Darrell squinted and raised his brow at the same time. "Uh, whut, are you talkin' 'bout, Son?" he asked, lifting the bill of his baseball cap and scratching his thick matted hair.

"I, I, I, you, I mean, the raven stabbed my hand, twice, and then stole my yo-yo, and, and, then you and the other one . . . was that mom? Uh, helped eat all of the, well at least some of the garbage in Ataya Lake, so the Shadows could have a proper burial . . ."

Degu's voiced trailed off as he saw his dad's eyes nearly bulging. The eyes were the perfect complement to the smirk spreading across his dad's face. Darrell covered his mouth with his hand to suppress his laugh.

By this time Honey was standing at the head of the dim hallway, one shoulder leaning against the wall, fingers scissored around the cigarette in her mouth, with a hand anchored on her other hip.

"Boy, that fever you had the past five days done messed up your mind. Maybe we need to take you down to the nuthouse and get you a room next to your grandmother."

In his mind, Degu heard the deep, clear voice of Talanuwa repeating the words from Rojo's note:

'Silence will serve you now.'

Darrell ambled past Honey and into the kitchen. He dropped the suitcase and stood with his hand clamped around the metal arc at the top of one of the vinyl kitchen chairs. "That boy was on me like white on rice. I never seen such a thing."

Honey looked over her shoulder at her husband and then returned her gaze to Degu. "Son, when you got sick, your grandmother went and got all crazy out in the middle of the street. She did her dance and pulled her pants down, squatted and peed on herself again; only this time, there was a policeman passing by."

Honey let out a tittering laugh. "She done got herself hauled off to the state mental hospital."

Darrell choked out a chuckle while Honey continued.

"You've been so sick with that fever, that we ain't bothered to tell you. Course, the good news is, since she went all loony out in public, the state is now going to pay for her time in the hospital."

Honey raised her hands above her head and twirled around. "We ain't got to pay one dime. Whohoo!"

She sauntered into the kitchen and wrapped her arms around Darrell. They did a celebratory tango twirl.

Degu pressed down the hallway and stood staring at his parents. "I, I, I—"

"I whut, Boy? Spit it out!" mocked Darrell.

Degu sucked in a deep breath and focused. He knew he couldn't remain silent. He brought to mind the Talanuwa's earlier counsel about his voice.

'You will need to learn how and when to use it.'

He now understood the balance of using his voice and using his silence. He slowed and spoke in a steadier and more deliberate tone.

"You've got El-li-si's suitcase. If you're going to see her, can I come?"

Darrell and Honey, still in their ballroom embrace, faced toward one another. "Whatcha think, babe?" Honey asked through another giggle.

"Well, I reckon his fever broke, since he's got all this energy. I don't believe I heard him talk this much in a month of Sundays. Course, he's doin' some crazy talk himself. What if they decide to keep him too?"

Honey scrunched her face in a faux frown and swatted Darrell on the chest. "Oh, now that's enough! You're gonna give that boy an even bigger complex than he already has." She pushed away from Darrell and sat back down at the table. She picked up her paper and returned to the store ads she was perusing.

Darrell shrugged his shoulders. "Alright, son. Let's go," he said, picking up the suitcase. Before turning toward the front door, Darrell reached down and tickled Honey on the ribs. "Don't you go throwin' no wild parties while I'm gone. Ya hear?"

"Ah!! Stop that now! Go on and go see your crazy mama. Git!"

Chapter 20

The drive to the state hospital brought Degu back into his usual silent form. His dad stared at the road ahead, never looking at his son, never engaging him in conversation. Every now and then, Darrell would chuckle and wipe his hand across his face. However, as they neared the entrance to the hospital grounds, Darrell's expression took a more serious turn. By the time they pulled to a stop in the parking lot directly across from the faded two story brick building, he had become solemn and fidgety.

He spoke in a low voice, still not making eye contact with his son. "Uh, maybe you ought to take your grandmother's things in to her. I'm sure she'll be a wantin' to see you anyways. You know, since you didn't get to say goodbye to her and all."

Darrell pulled his balled fist up to his mouth and cleared his throat. His eyes moved in Degu's direction, but slightly down, never coming into full contact with Degu's. "Go on now. I'll be waitin' right here. You take as much time as you need."

Degu stared at his father briefly, then turned and reached into the back of the truck's cab to retrieve El-li-si's suitcase. He hesitated, opened his door and stepped out. Closing the door, he heard a rustle of wind through the trees. He looked up and saw another stately oak tree, with a stout trunk and a still-full canopy of red, yellow and orange leaves. The swaying leaves reminded Degu of their counterparts, the newly budding, light green shoots of leaves dancing on the tree in Ataya Lake. He felt for the small wooden yo-yo in his jeans pocket. Squeezing it in the palm of his hand, Degu turned and walked towards the front steps of the old hospital building. At the base of the steps, he glanced up at the faded letters etched into the masonry facing atop the buildings dirty, white columns:

JAMES P. SOARING HALL

Degu ascended the stone steps, skipping several with each lengthy stride. The first thing he noticed when he crossed into the main lobby was the smell, a sweet, musky smell. He walked over to the reception desk and asked the petite, gray haired lady, busily typing.

"Excuse me, ma'am. I've brought some things for Ms. Ama Collins. May I go see her?"

The lady looked up from her computer screen and smiled under the half lens reading glasses sitting low on the bridge of her nose. "Sweetie, you must be talkin' 'bout Ms. El-li-si. She's been expectin' you."

The receptionist pushed a button on her phone and called for an escort. A short, stocky, olive-skinned man with wide set eyes, a broad flat nose and thick black hair parted in the middle came around the corner. He was dressed in jeans and a forest green hospital-issued uniform top.

Rock?

"You must be Degotoga. Follow me please."

"Uh, okay." Degu was perplexed. *How did they know that I was coming?*

He shuffled ahead to catch up to the man who was walking briskly, arms swinging widely by his side. The hospitals walls were beige and showed the wear of their age. Sporadically lining the walls at uneven heights was a series of cheap, plastic gold-framed pictures that were undeniably cut out of wildlife magazines. The creases still showed in some of them. The orderly whistled a tune that Degu strained to recognize.

Is that Scar Tissue by the Red Hot Chili Peppers?

He glanced at several of the pictures; a mountain lion, then a sheep; a young brown elk, then a timber wolf; a ball python and then a small gray mouse. They turned left down the first bisecting hallway and stopped at the first room on the right. At this point, Degu was not the least surprised at what he saw next to El-li-si's door: a picture of several turkey and black vultures keeping watch, sitting high in a dead tree.

The orderly rapped three times on the door. It was ajar, and creaked open several more inches. "Ms. El-li-si," his voice lifted and lilted. "Degotoga's here to see you."

The orderly took a step back into the middle of the hall and swung his arms, palms facing upwards in a motion for Degu to go ahead into the room. As Degu stepped through the doorway, the orderly turned and walked away, resuming his boisterous whistle.

The room was shadowy, like dusk. Degu peered around the corner of the small foyer space over towards the bed. It was fully made, with a few wrinkles. There was no initial sign of his grandmother. A slight breeze blew in on both the heavy brown vinyl curtain and the sheer white inner lining, their graceful wave betraying the fact that the window was open. Degu felt the cool air puff across his face. He set down his grandmother's suitcase and walked steadily over to pull the curtains back. Looking out he saw that there was at least a 30 foot drop to the ground.

There's no way she—

He saw a commotion out of the corner of his eye and looked up to see a lone vulture slowing into a landing on what looked like his dad's old stand in the oak tree next to the parking lot. This creature brought to mind all of the encounters in the Adanvado.

Degu smiled. *Is it you, El-li-si?*

The majestic bird stared intently at him and then turned and began scrapping its harshly hooked beak on the wooden planks of the stand.

Degu, still grinning, turned and walked out of the room and down the hall towards the front of the building. The receptionist was fussing with a phone call while the orderly was busy preparing medication doses to give the patients. He strode directly out without speaking to either as they both paused from their duties to watch him pass. He moved casually down the steps and in the direction of his dad's old pickup truck. The cab was empty. Sitting on the top was a sleek black raven that bobbed his head several times as Degu walked by.

He walked over to the massive oak tree that held the tree stand. He instinctively looked around to the back side. There was the knotted rope hanging from one of the first branches. Degu wrapped his hands around and began to shimmy up and into the tree. His chest expanded in certainty with each branch ascended. While pulling himself up and onto the tree stand, two more vultures, one red and one black, floated in and landed, one on each side of him. He sat cross-legged as the black vulture leaned in and rested her head on his thigh. The turkey vulture lifted a foot and placed it on his other thigh. Before him, Degu saw his familiar sketches along with the words, *Madness*, *Roots*, and *Soaring*. Below these words, he saw what the El-li-si had been scratching:

Home

Epilogue (A Cherokee Legend)

A long time ago, when the Cherokee newly walked upon the earth, they didn't like the darkness and decided that they would be happier if there were no night. They prayed to Ouga, the Creator, and asked for constant daylight, no darkness. Ouga heard their voices and answered their prayers.

There was no more darkness. Soon, the woodlands and the fields became heavy with growth. It became too difficult to walk the lands. The people toiled long and hard in the gardens and fields, trying to keep weeds from strangling the corn, tomatoes and other plants. It became so very hot, and remained so day after day after day. The Cherokee also found it hard to sleep in the constant light and became quarrelsome with one another.

Many days passed before the people realized the foolishness of their plea. They went again in prayer, beseeching the Creator. "O Great Ouga, our vision was short and foolish in asking that it be day all of the time. We now ask of you that it be night always." The Creator considered this new request and decided that, although all things were created in twos, abundance and want, life and death, good and evil, Ouga decided to grant their request.

The day was no more. Night covered the earth. The crops stopped growing as the cold and darkness settled in. The people could not see to hunt game. They spent much of their time gathering wood for fires. Soon, they became cold and very weak. Many of the Cherokee died.

The remaining peoples gathered together, beseeching the Creator. They cried out, "O Great Ouga! We have been blind and foolish, and did not know of what we asked you. You are the Creator of all that is, and you have made everything perfect from the beginning; day and night as they should be. We pray that you forgive us our ignorance and make the day and night as they were before."

Once more the Creator listened to and heeded the request of the people. The day and night were restored, as they had been from the beginning of time; light and dark in perfect balance. The weather improved and the crops began to grow again. Hunting again flourished as there was an abundance of game. The Cherokee had plenty to eat and there was less sickness. The people were kind and generous with one another. Life was good and the people offered their gratitude to Ouga.

Ouga accepted their expressions of thanksgiving and was pleased to see their joy return. However, because of the long period of nights that caused so many deaths, the Creator was aggrieved. Ouga placed the spirits of the deceased in a newly created tree. The tree was named a-tsi-na tlu gv, the cedar tree.

When you smell the aroma or gaze upon an honorable cedar standing in the forest, remember that, if you are Cherokee, you are beholding your ancestor.

And finally, a blessing to all tribes:

When you come into the presence of the oak, remember that, no matter your tribe, you are beholding the spirit of great courage and power. May the Mighty Oak that lives inside of you, anchor you and keep you through all of life's travels and travails.

ACKNOWLEDGEMENTS

While writing is always a labor of love for me, it's most comforting to know that I have a steady and supportive cohort to keep me balanced with sage advice and feedback. In particular, I would like to thank my fellow authors Tony Bowman and P.T. McHugh for their reads and thorough critiques of my early drafts. Your insights made this a much better book. I would also like to thank the Holly Springs Writers Guild Critique Group for their enthusiasm and gentle feedback. It's a great thing to be in the midst of folks who are passionate about writing. Finally, I would like to thank Ginny Vaca and La Vonne Brown for their steadfast support of all of my writing projects. You've been my best cheerleaders from day one. Thank you Ginny and La Vonne!

ABOUT THE AUTHOR

Hugh J Willard is a writer and psychotherapist living and working in Holly Springs, NC. He has previously authored several childrens' books including Alphatorts; and The Goodwill Vulture's Club Series. You can learn more about Hugh by going to www.HughWillard.com